RESCUE BY NIGHT

Fargo rose to a crouch, knew they'd not pick him out against the blackness of the trees. He moved with the two figures, step by shuffling step, stayed abreast of them as they neared the horses. There would be a few precious seconds when the one pushed Linda onto the horse. He would have to pull the gun from her head to get her into the saddle.

Fargo was directly opposite the two men as they reached the horses, the Colt raised in his hand. The mustached one with Linda pushed her against his horse, reached down and grabbed her by one leg, half lifted and half threw her up into the saddle. But his gun was not against her temple. The vital seconds were there. Fargo fired the shot, a single shot . . .

A GIANT TRAILSMAN

THE

TRAILSMAN

#200

SPECIAL
ANNIVERSARY
EDITION

SIX-GUNS
BY SEA

by

Jon Sharpe

A SIGNET BOOK

SIGNET
Published by the Penguin Group
Penguin Putnam Inc., 375 Hudson Street,
New York, New York 10014, U.S.A.
Penguin Books Ltd, 27 Wrights Lane,
London W8 5TZ, England
Penguin Books Australia Ltd,
Ringwood, Victoria, Australia
Penguin Books Canada Ltd, 10 Alcorn Avenue,
Toronto, Ontario, Canada M4V 3B2
Penguin Books (N.Z.) Ltd, 182-190 Wairau Road,
Auckland 10, New Zealand

Penguin Books Ltd, Registered Offices:
Harmondsworth, Middlesex, England

Published by Signet, an imprint of Dutton NAL,
a member of Penguin Putnam Inc.

First Printing, August, 1998
10 9 8 7 6 5 4 3 2 1

Copyright © Jon Sharpe, 1998
All rights reserved

The first chapter of this book originally appeared in *Wyoming Wildcats*,
the one hundred ninety-ninth volume in this series.

 REGISTERED TRADEMARK—MARCA REGISTRADA

Printed in the United States of America

The Trailsman

Beginnings . . . they bend the tree and they mark the man. Skye Fargo was born when he was eighteen. Terror was his midwife, vengeance his first cry. Killing spawned Skye Fargo, ruthless, cold-blooded murder. Out of the acrid smoke of gunpowder still hanging in the air, he rose, cried out a promise never forgotten.

The Trailsman they began to call him all across the West: searcher, scout, hunter, the man who could see where others only looked, his skills for hire but not his soul, the man who lived each day to the fullest, yet trailed each tomorrow. Skye Fargo, the Trailsman, and the seeker who could take the wildness of a land and the wanting of a woman and make them his own.

Some of the real-life figures who have stepped from history into the pages of this story:

Congressman James Murray Mason:
 Arrested in 1861 on a British merchantman on his way to London with Senator John Slidell.

Senator John Slidell:
 Once the American negotiator during the Mexican War.

William L. Yancey:
 Wealthy businessman turned politician.

Prince Napoleon:
 Special envoy to the United States from the French government.

Camille Ferri Pisano:
 Aide-de-camp to Prince Napoleon.

General Pierre Gustave Toutant Beauregard:
 Resigned as superintendent of West Point, became commander under Robert E. Lee. The only Creole general in the United States Army.

John Wilkes Booth:
   Assassinated President Lincoln. Killed by U.S. troops.
Lewis Powell aka Payne:
   Eventually executed by hanging as conspirator in assassination of President Lincoln.
David Herold:
   Helped John Wilkes Booth escape. Hanged as conspirator in assassination of President Lincoln.
George Atzenrodt:
   German immigrant secessionist spy, eventually hanged as conspirator in assassination of President Lincoln.
Mary Surratt:
   Provided house for plot against President Lincoln. Eventually hanged as conspirator, along with Powell, Herold, and Atzenrodt.
Captain John Winslow, USN:
   Commanded federal sloop *Kearsage* that sank the notorious Confederate raider *Alabama* off the coast of Cherbourg, France, after the *Alabama* had sunk sixty merchantmen.
John Nicolay:
   Secretary and confidant to Abraham Lincoln.
Abraham Lincoln:
   Sixteenth president of the United States.

*1860, where Kentucky and Virginia
pressed against the towering strength
of the Appalachian range, when hate
and death cast their shadows over
a growing nation, from purple mountains
majesty to shining seas . . .*

1

The big man's lake blue eyes narrowed as he peered at the four horsemen who rode on the ridge just below him. He moved the Ovaro slowly, held the horse almost at a walk as the four riders moved back and forth, plainly searching the dense foliage. The late afternoon sun came in at a slant through the red cedar and the shagbark hickory to paint the ground with long streaks of gold that made the riders pass from light into shadow. They moved forward in a straight line, kept some dozen feet from one another, leaning from their saddles as they used their rifles to poke and prod the dense brush. They had no easy searching. Whether one trespassed through the Alleghenies, the Blue Ridge Mountains or the Shenandoah Valley, the Appalachians hid everything in their thick, lush, verdant cloak.

White ash, red cedar, sycamore, hawthorn and hemlock, joe-pye weed, moth mullein, broomsedge and beggarweed, blue grass, witchgrass, and bristle-grass, the dark green, shiny, thick leaves of rhododendron, the flame of azalea, the lemon of the evening primrose and rose purple of bull thistle all grew together—commingling, intertwining, creating a vast leafy carpet side by side, around, and atop one another, a profusion of greenery that was both welcoming and forbidding. Above it all, yet part of it, towered the vast mountains of the Appalachians. Skye Fargo touched the flank of the Ovaro with his left knee and sent the horse down an opening between ranks of red cedar that led to the ridge below and the four riders.

They looked at him as he pushed through the trees into the relative open of the ridge and reined up at once. "Where'd you come from, mister?" one of them asked, a burly man with a broad-cheekboned face and a bristly red mustache.

"On the ridge above you," Fargo said pleasantly, and his eyes took in the four men in a single glance, saw hard-jawed, stern faces.

"You see a man running on foot?" the red-mustached one asked.

"No, but it's plain you're looking for somebody," Fargo said.

"Runaway prisoner," one of the others said, a thin-faced man with piercing eyes.

"You lawmen?" Fargo asked, keeping his tone bland.

"That's right," the man answered.

"Don't see any badges," Fargo remarked casually.

"Take our word for it," the man said and moved his horse forward. "We've got a prisoner to find," he muttered, and the four men began their search once again, moving in unison. Fargo kept his horse in place and watched the men ride on and call to each other. "Spread out more," the mustached one said. "Goddammit, where's the damn blood? There's got to be a blood trail. You know we got him. His saddle was covered with blood."

"I tell you he's lying dead someplace. We just can't see him in this goddamn place," another put in.

"We keep looking," the first one returned, and they went on out of sight into a thick part of the wooded ridge.

"Amateurs," Fargo hissed disdainfully. Automatically, his eyes swept the thick, dense greenery. But it was no ordinary glance. These were the eyes that had learned to see as the hawk sees, to probe as the fox probes, to focus as the mountain lion focuses. These eyes could measure the way of a trail, a sign, a mark, a man, or a maid. These were the eyes of the Trailsman, and behind each lake blue orb lay the wisdom and the lore of the land and all its ways. With it came that special instinct born of the wild and touched by the wind, that sixth sense that went beyond all other senses.

The four men were no lawmen, no deputies. They hadn't the look of lawmen. They had the look of hunters tracking their prey. Skye Fargo grimaced. He'd come a long way to reach the mighty Appalachians. It had been a good while since he had ridden these almost impenetrable mountains, and he wasn't inclined to poke into things not of his concern. Besides, he had someplace to be and was barely on schedule. Nosing the Ovaro forward into the denseness of a thicket of red cedar, he found himself thinking about the letter in his pocket.

It had summoned him all the way from the Great Plains of the West. The money that had come with it was already safe in a bank in Minnesota. It was the kind of money no sane man would turn down, the letter no more cryptic than others he'd received in the past. Men who wanted a new trail broken had a tendency to be cryptic, he had learned over the years. Secrecy seemed a part of their thinking, as if a trail could be kept secret. He'd just finished breaking a new trail near the Overland route, and he'd left Kansas when the letter had arrived. He'd ridden the long miles leisurely and swung north only when he reached Kentucky, that land the Indian Chief Dragging Canoe had aptly named the "dark and bloody ground." Riding over land that cradled the beginnings of America, he turned south when he reached Boone's trace, where, less than a hundred years before, Daniel Boone had carved a path out of the wilderness.

It was this path that Boone took westward, across the Ohio and into Indiana and the untamed West beyond. Fargo had stayed south, took the Cumberland Gap, then rode north into the Appalachians as he decided to get in some early exploring of his own. He was still retracing his route in his mind when a sound cut into his thoughts. He halted, pushed aside a leafy branch, and saw a lone rider following the path the four men had taken. He frowned for a moment. This rider was a slender figure with dark blond hair cut short, a red-and-black checkered shirt, and Levi's. But she searched the dense brush and scanned the trees just as the four men had done.

He watched as she leaned first right and then left out of the saddle as she slowly moved a dish-faced mare. She cupped a hand around her mouth to direct her calls in a hoarse whisper. "Kenny, it's me," she called. "Can you hear me? Are you there?" She paused, then moved on, peering into the denseness of brush, bushes, weeds, and trees, calling out again.

Fargo moved out of the cedars, let her see him, and she pulled up, alarm flooding her face at once. He saw her hand go to her belt, where she had a Starr, double-action, six-shot Navy revolver.

He nodded calmly at her. "You looking for the same escaped prisoner those other fellers are looking for?" he asked.

"Is that who they said they're looking for?" she answered.

"Yep. You?" he asked again.

"I don't know," the young woman said, and Fargo's brows lifted, the answer not one he expected. She had dark blue eyes set in a face more pleasant than pretty, yet with nice full lips, a wide mouth, and a small nose.

"You don't know?" he echoed. "What's that mean?"

"I'm looking for my brother, Kenny," she said.

"What made you come here looking for him?"

"Been doing it for the last three days. Kenny usually visits at this time of the month. I rode up, saw

15

those four, and got really frightened. I heard them say they'd shot somebody," the young woman said.

"What makes you think it was your brother they shot?" Fargo asked.

"Damn few folks would be coming up here. I knew Kenny was due. Maybe they're dry-gulchers that jumped him," she said.

Fargo's lips pursed. "Not likely," he murmured.

"Why not?" She frowned.

"Dry-gulchers look for a quick hit, usually. That means they go where they have opportunities, outside a town, a stage route, places well traveled. They wouldn't come looking for a victim in these godforsaken mountains," Fargo said.

"They shot somebody. They're trying to find a blood trail," she said.

"I know. I heard," he said.

"It could have been Kenny," she insisted. "I want to be sure. I'm going to keep looking—for whoever it is."

"And making the same mistakes they are," he said.

"How?" She frowned.

"You're looking for blood on the tops of leaves and bushes, just as they are."

"That's where it'd be," she said.

"If he's running," Fargo said. "That's when a wounded man will drop blood on the tops of leaves and bushes. If he's crawling, he'll leave a blood trail on the underside of leaves and long stems."

"You think he's crawling?" she asked, her blue eyes wide.

"I'd bet on it," Fargo said.

"How do you know so much?" the young woman asked.

"Name's Fargo, Skye Fargo. Some call me the Trailsman," he said.

"Linda Corrigan," she said. "Help me look. Please. It could be my brother. Maybe he got into a fight with them."

Fargo let a sigh escape his lips as he swung from the saddle and started to walk across the ground at right angles to where the four men had searched. As he went into a crouch and began to part brush, leaves, and bushes, he saw her slide from her horse and begin to search as he did. But Fargo didn't search for blood at first as his eyes scoured leaves and stems, weeds, flowers, bushes. Suddenly, he found what he sought, stems and leaves that were bruised near their base. The spots of blood came quickly after that. "Over here," he called as he pushed on, staying in a crouch. Linda Corrigan was hurrying toward him when he saw the figure lying facedown in thick shrubbery. He knelt beside it, turned the figure on its back, and saw a young man half conscious with the same dark blond hair that Linda Corrigan had. The man was bleeding heavily from a hole through his throat.

"Oh, God. Oh, God. It's Kenny," Linda said as she reached him, dropping to one knee beside him.

"He's still alive, but that's a nasty wound," Fargo said.

"We have to stop the bleeding," she said, her hands tearing at the red-and-black checkered shirt. She pulled it off, and Fargo saw she wore a camisole underneath that clung to small, upturned breasts that pressed into the thin fabric. He helped her wrap the shirtsleeves around the young man's neck.

"I'll finish. Get your horse," he said.

"I've a cabin. Help me get him there," she said, and Fargo finished wrapping the makeshift bandage as she rose and ran back to the gray mare. She returned in moments, and Fargo carefully lifted the limp figure onto her horse and placed him on his stomach as Linda swung onto the saddle behind him.

"Slowly, real slowly," Fargo said as he went back to the Ovaro and rode behind her as she climbed a narrow trail up to the ridge above. Once on the ridge, she turned west, and he rode beside her. She had a firm, lean figure, nice strong shoulders, and the smallish breasts hardly moved as she rode—everything about her tight and lean.

"Bastards," she murmured through tight lips. "Whoever they are." He didn't answer and turned the question in his mind. No dry-gulchers, he reiterated silently. And no chance meeting that resulted in an argument. They'd have left him for dead and gone their way. But these men searched after him, were still searching, purposeful, determined to finish him. They had reasons, and Fargo glanced at Linda Corrigan and wondered how much she knew about her brother. She rode with her jaw set, and in her dark blue eyes he saw pain and anger.

"You know any reasons why they'd want to shoot your brother?" he asked.

"He was into something. He wouldn't tell me what," Linda Corrigan said. "Maybe he will now."

"You were very close?" Fargo asked.

"When he was growing up, he was a great kid brother," she said, then fell silent with her own thoughts. He tabled asking more, but wondered what she was doing up here in the wildness of the Blue Ridge Mountains. The sun still found its way through the towering sycamores, bitternut, and black oak, and Fargo saw a road suddenly appear and curve around a high hill. He rounded the curve with Linda, and the cabin appeared. Only it was more of a long log house than a cabin, with a smaller structure alongside it.

Fronting the house a long stretch of canvas attached to tall poles afforded a cover that plainly could be rolled partly or completely back. Beneath the canvas roof were rows of clay pots and long wooden boxes, all with plants growing in them. A workbench to one side was covered with glass vials containing seeds. He was staring at everything as Linda drew up in front of the house, where the door hung open. Dismounting, Fargo lifted the unconscious form from the horse and followed Linda into the house, where he saw a large room comfortably furnished with a sofa, chairs, and dining table. A cot rested against one wall, and he lowered Kenny Corrigan onto it. Linda immediately loosened the makeshift bandage around her brother's neck. Blood began flowing from the wound at once, and Linda disappeared, then returned with a proper bandage and wrapped it around the man's neck. She turned to Fargo and met his eyes. "It won't do, will it?" she said.

"No. He needs a doc and fast," Fargo said.

"We'll take him to Pine Hollow. It's at the foot of the mountain," Linda said.

"There's a doc up here in these mountains?" Fargo frowned.

"Doc Benson," she said. "There are mountain people up here, families, that need tending to. Then there are trappers, hunters, and woodsmen who get themselves hurt in one way or another. He's no fancy hospital doctor, but he manages. Real serious cases he can't handle he sends down to Virginia, if they can make it. There's a hospital at Roanoke. I'll use my wagon. Kenny won't make it by horse."

She went off, returned in a moment with a green shirt on, and he followed her outside to the rear of the house, where he saw an Owensboro huckster wagon with flare board sides and a drop end-gate.

He helped her hitch the gray mare to the wagon. "There's only one road down," she said as he carried the unconscious form from the house and laid it on a blanket she had spread in the wagon. She climbed onto the seat and took the reins. "Want me to come along?" he asked.

Her hand touched his arm and stayed there. "I'd like that," she said, her blue eyes grave. "If it weren't for you, he might still be back there dead. You can leave your horse. He'll find the oat bin around back."

"You can be sure of that," Fargo said and pulled himself onto the seat beside her. He glanced again at the canvas-roofed area and the rows of clay pots as she drove past. "What is all this?" he asked. "And what are you doing up here in the middle of the Appalachians? You're no mountain girl."

"I sometimes think I'm becoming one," she said. "I'm a botanist. I'm making a listing and a study of every variety of plant, flower, shrub, seed, and tree in the mountains, starting here in the Blue Ridge. The state of Virginia gave me a grant to do it. It'll be the only study of its kind. It'll take years to finish, of course."

"Then you don't spend all your time up here in the mountains."

"I try to get away every month or two for a few days," she said.

"Where?"

"A family house in Virginia, north of Shenandoah. It lets me visit Fredericksburg or Alexandria," Linda said. "Lets me visit the social scene."

"You're an unusual combination of things, I'd say," Fargo remarked.

"I get caught up in whatever I do, my work or whatever is important to me," Linda said. "Why are you here, Fargo?"

"I'm on my way to see a man who wants me to break a new trail through the Appalachians," he told her.

She let her dark blue eyes study him for a long, thoughtful moment. "I imagine you'll do it," she said. "And I'll be sort of sorry."

"Sorry?" He frowned.

"I like the Appalachians the way they are, majestic, unspoiled, uncontaminated, no man-made trails, no incursions by hordes of people."

"Or cattle," he said.

"Or cattle," she agreed.

"You may have it your way," he said, his eyes going to the towering green peaks. "These are formidable mountains. They're beautiful and forbidding." His words ended as dusk began to lower, enshrouding the tall peaks. The road turned and twisted, but Linda drove well, handled the wagon with ease. An unusual and complicated young woman, he decided, with her own, understated attractiveness. Night had descended over the Appalachians when they reached Pine Hollow, a cleared circle of land at the foot of three mountains and surrounded by Virginia pine, fragrant with their short needles and prickly cones. Doc Benson's quarters consisted of two almost identical houses that turned out to be primitively equipped, yet neat and clean.

Doc Benson greeted them as they drove up, a tall, spare man with a face both ascetic and strong. A woman with her hair pulled back and wearing a white apron stood by. The doctor looked at Kenny Corrigan and helped Fargo move him inside to a clean bed, where he examined the young man more carefully. "He's lost a lot of blood, too much," the doctor told Linda. "I'll try to bring him around. Meanwhile, I'll put a tube into that hole in his throat to stop him from losing more blood and dissipating air. I think you should come back in the morning."

"You don't sound hopeful," Linda said.

"I'm not," Doc Benson said honestly. "If we can get him stabilized, we can try getting him to Roanoke."

"I'll be back in the morning," Linda said. "Do your best. But I know you'll do that," she added. She took hold of Fargo's arm as she walked into the night and paused at the carriage.

"Want me to drive?" he asked, and she nodded.

"Just follow the road," she said, and he took the reins. She sat close beside him, and the moon came up to light the road as it curved and twisted its way upward. She rode in silence until they returned to her place, where she hurried inside first and lighted two kerosene lamps. "The cabin alongside the house is for guests. I'd like you to stay the night. I owe you. Kenny owes you," she said. "There's a covered stable in the back. That's a fine Ovaro, too fine to leave out all night."

"I'll stay. I'm feeling the ride over here," Fargo said. She handed him one of the lamps, and he took it, then went outside, unsaddled and stabled the pinto in a small, three-horse structure that was sturdier than it appeared at first sight. He went to the smaller cabin at the end of the house and found it clean, a dresser and good-sized bed against one wall, a reed rug on the floor. He began to undress and was down to his trousers when he heard footsteps at the door. Linda came in carrying a small tray with sandwiches and a coffee mug.

"Thought you could use something to eat," she said and set the tray down on a small end table. She wore a short, knee-length blue nightdress that made her look almost little girllike as it clung to her small breasts and lay against her slender body.

"Thanks," he said and saw her eyes travel slowly across the muscled beauty of his torso. As she lowered herself to the edge of the bed, he felt her eyes staying on him. "I feel as though I'm one of the seeds you study." He smiled.

"Sorry." She laughed softly. "I was just wondering if all trailsmen are as uncommonly handsome as you."

"You've been alone in these mountains too long," he said.

"Probably," she agreed. "Maybe it's made me restless, but not blind."

"One thing affects another," he said and laughed between bites of the sandwich.

"Not with me. I'm a scientist. I know about keeping things separate," she said.

"I imagine you do," he said honestly. "You keep your own contrasts separated, too, I'll wager."

"What contrasts?" she questioned.

"The botanist, the young woman scientist, the dedicated professional, and the little girl look-alike in that nightdress," he said.

A slow smile spread across her wide mouth, reluctant admiration curled inside it. "You're very astute," she murmured.

"I read signs, remember?" he said, finishing the meal.

She rose, came to stand before him, and placed both

24

hands on the muscled smoothness of his chest. Her lips lifted and came to his, lingered, soft and warm, and her breath came in short gasps until finally she pulled away, her fingers curling against his naked torso. "How do you read that?" she asked softly. "Scientist or little girl?"

"Maybe some of both," he said.

"You're wrong about both. It was a simple thank-you for helping me," she said.

He smiled. "Bullshit, honey," he said.

She gave a little shrug with her half smile, turned away, and glided from the cabin. "Good night, Fargo," she called back.

He laughed as he finished undressing and lay down on the bed. His thoughts stayed on her before he closed his eyes. Her quiet pleasantness was deceptive. Behind that first impression was an undoubtedly brilliant young woman. Maybe there was a little girl behind the dedicated botanist. Designers were fond of saying form should follow function. Nature had been doing that for millenniums. The design of every flower, plant, tree, and rock fitted its function. But sometimes nature disguised function with form, played its own tricks. Were there two Linda Corrigans, he wondered, or one simply in disguise. He let the smile stay with him as sleep came and the night grew still.

He didn't know how long he'd slept, at least a few hours, when his wild creature hearing set him awake. He sat up, listened, and heard the sounds, shuffling footsteps, a muffled cry. He swung long legs from the bed, pulled on trousers and gun belt, and swung the cabin door open. The sounds were suddenly less muffled, a man's voice. "Where is he, goddammit?" the questioner rasped, followed by the sound of a slap and Linda's short cry of pain. "You got him here, dammit."

"No," Linda murmured.

Fargo went into the night, crouched, and started for the house. "Look in that other cabin," a man said, and Fargo recognized the voice of the man with the bristly mustache. Dropping to one knee, Fargo raised the Colt, then lowered it. He could bring them down easily as they charged toward the cabin, but that would leave the others holding Linda. They'd not hesitate to kill her, he knew. He backed quickly into the deepest shadows at the rear of the small cabin as the door of the house opened and the two figures charged out.

They headed for the cabin, and Fargo cursed softly. They'd see clothes, the rumpled bed, and assume Kenny had run out. They'd shout the alarm to the house. It could be enough for the others to shoot Linda. Fargo cursed again. He had to take out the two men and do it silently. The throwing knife lay in its calf holster under the bed, and he swore as he stayed on one knee, letting his hand grope along the ground. The two men reached the cabin door as his hand suddenly halted, his fingers touching something smooth, hard, and curved. A rock, he thought at first, then ran his fingers across the object, frowned as he felt it taper outward at the top. He closed his hand around it, lifted, and saw it was one of Linda's clay pots. It

26

would have to do, he thought. Perhaps it was only fitting. The two men charged into the cabin, and he lay the Colt on the ground beside his knee. He'd have to move with split-second timing and absolute accuracy, he knew.

Gathering his muscles, nerves, and the combination of all the senses called marksmanship, he waited, his arm upraised, the clay pot clutched in his hand. The two men raced from the cabin in seconds, starting toward the house. But the clay pot was already hurtling through the air, its smooth, curved contours offering almost no wind friction. Fargo saw it smash into the first of the two men before he'd taken three steps from the doorway, smashing into pieces as it struck. The man collapsed on the spot, as though his legs had suddenly evaporated, and he crumpled to the ground. The other man turned to stare at him in surprise, frowning, taking precious seconds to comprehend what had happened. When he finally tore his eyes away from the crumpled figure, he looked up, but the Colt was whistling toward him. He saw it too late as it materialized out of the darkness, hurtling end over end. The butt smashed into his forehead, and Fargo heard a faint cracking sound.

The man staggered and collapsed, hitting the ground only seconds before Fargo reached him. Scooping up the Colt, Fargo started for the house, then halted as the voice came. "What's taking Jake and Benny so goddamn long?" it asked.

"Somethin's wrong," the mustached man snarled. Fargo heard him drag Linda with him as he made for the door. Flattening himself on the ground, Fargo rolled almost to the trees, then stayed on the ground, but with a better view of the doorway. The two men emerged together, both with revolvers raised. The mustached one had an arm around Linda's neck, the gun held to her head. "One shot and she's dead," he shouted. Fargo swore under his breath. He couldn't risk a shot in the half-light from the doorway. Even if he hit his target, the man's finger would pull the trigger in a reflex action. Fargo lay silently as the two men moved together across the open ground toward the horses a dozen feet away. Both were nervous, he knew, both peering into the night as they pushed Linda to the horses with them.

They'd take her with them, and it'd be at least a minute before he could get to the Ovaro in the stable. They might hang onto her as a hostage or discard her with a bullet. Either way she faced certain death. Fargo rose to a crouch. He knew they'd not pick him out against the blackness of the trees. He moved with the two figures, step by shuffling step, stayed abreast of them as they neared the horses. There'd be a few precious seconds when one pushed Linda onto the horse. He'd have to pull the gun from her head to get her into the saddle.

Fargo was directly opposite the two men as they reached the horses, the Colt raised in his hand. The mustached one with Linda pushed her against his horse, then reached down and grabbed her by one leg, half lifted half threw her up into the saddle. But his gun was not against her temple. The vital seconds were there. Fargo fired the Colt, a single shot. The mustached man whirled, fell backward against his horse, and stayed there until the animal bolted. He slid to the ground in a heap, and Fargo saw Linda leap from the saddle and hit the ground on her hands and knees. He also saw the last man astride his horse, sending the animal racing into the darkness.

Fargo ran past Linda as she pushed herself up and leaped on the other horse. "No loose ends," he tossed at her as he spurred the horse forward. He picked up the fleeing rider at once, the man racing down the twisting wagon path. Fargo wished he rode the Ovaro as the horse plodded after the other animal. But the fleeing rider was trying too hard, his horse taking the curves too wide, the animal overstriding as the man pushed it instead of collecting its motion. Fargo saw he was gaining, drew closer, and waited for the next twisting curve to appear. When it did, the fleeing rider flew around it, presenting himself sideways for an instant. It was enough. Fargo fired and saw the man sail from the horse, smashing onto the ground in a tangle of arms and legs, then lying still.

Fargo walked the horse to the figure, peered down at it for another moment, then turned the horse and rode back to the house. As he approached, he saw Linda in the doorway, the revolver in her hand. She ran toward him as she recognized him, and he swung to the ground in time to catch her as she flung herself against him, her arms wrapped around his neck. She clung to him as a wet leaf clings to a rock, and he felt the small points press into his chest with firm round-ness.

"I never thought they'd come up here looking," she said.

"They must want Kenny very badly," Fargo said. "There has to be a reason. What did he have, or what did he know?" She shrugged helplessly and stepped back, her eyes wide. "I think you'd best find out, for your own protection."

"I will, I will," Linda said.

"This much is over," he said reassuringly.

"Stay with me, Fargo. I don't want to be alone," she said.

"Sure thing," he said, and her hand curled around his. She led him into the adjoining room, where he saw the large bed fluffed with pillows. Her hand was still holding his as she reached the bed and pulled him onto it with her. Her eyes roamed across his face, down to his chest as he felt her hands tugging at his gun belt, then his trousers. He shed both and watched as, on both knees, she faced him, lifted the short nightgown, and tossed it over her head.

He felt the sharp intake of breath and the rush of surprise that swept through him. He felt not unlike a collector who'd come upon a gem of unexpected beauty, a small but totally entrancing find. She stayed very straight and very still, showing herself for him, enjoying the appreciation in his eyes. He savored the moment. It was worth savoring. The small breasts fit perfectly with the rest of her, and they thrust upward with insouciance, almost impudence. Each sharp little pink nipple seemed to reach up from its soft pink circle, and below her breasts a lean chest and narrow waist curved beautifully down to narrow hips and a flat, almost concave little belly.

Just below that a small triangle rose up, almost devoid of anything but a soft fuzz, yet entirely in keeping with the rest of her. He took in legs that were lean yet not without lovely lines, thighs filling out where they touched each other. The little-girl look clung to her, he noted, but now it melded with a simmering womanliness. He reached out. It was time to stop looking—time to find out about contrasts.

2

Linda came forward to meet Fargo's touch, and he cupped the pert, upturned breasts in his hands, feeling their delicious, soft firmness. He lay down with her, and his eyes stayed on the two sharply pointed nipples, provocative in their very shape and thrust, insouciant beauty asking to be caressed. He ran his thumb across the tiny point of one, brought his lips down to the other, and Linda Corrigan shuddered as she squealed with delight. He let his lips pull gently on the upturned, saucy mound, drawing it deeper into his mouth, and his tongue circled the pink areola, slowly, touch savoring touch as the little point grew firmer and responded at once. Linda's cries rose, short, sharp gasps, and he felt her body lifting, pushing against him.

But there was no slow surging for her, her lithe, lean body coming hard against his—little sharp movements, soft poundings of her breasts against him, her stomach into his groin. "Oh, jeez, oh, God, oh, yes, yes, yes," Linda gasped out, and her hands began to travel up and down his body, small, fluttery motions down along his ribs, his chest, down to his groin as short, sharp sounds came from her. Her fingers slid downward across his muscled abdomen, down farther, and her body continued to push hard into his. When she closed her fingers around the hot, pulsating maleness of him, she gave a long scream, and her head fell back, neck arching, mouth open. "Aiiiieeee . . . oh, yes, yes, oh, God," she called out, and suddenly seemed to leap forward. She rubbed her body against his, each motion short, almost harsh, then she rolled and took him with her, came atop him.

He watched the small breasts bounce firmly up and down as she straddled him. "Easy, there . . . easy," he murmured, but she would have no part of that, and her hard, bouncing, bucking motions grew stronger. Her lean thighs lifted, came against his hips, and she fell forward over him, thrusting the bouncing breasts into his face.

"Take me, take me, take me," she gasped as her thighs opened and closed against him, a franticness to her, desire ahead of itself, frenzy almost out of control. He closed his hands around her small waist, turned her with him, pressed her down on the bed, and placed one hand over her pubic mound and held it there, pressing firmly, and she suddenly grew still, a soft moan coming from her. "Ah . . . aaaaah," she breathed, and he kept the flat of his palm over the small rise of her Venus mound, slowly rubbing, fingers pushing no fibrous, dense nap but only a soft, fuzzlike covering. She sighed again, and her hands moved down along his body, firmly but less frantically. He moved and brought himself over her, slowly lifting his palm from the roundness of her little mound, then slid his hand downward and felt the sudden dampness of her. He slid down farther, and Linda began to tremble again. The little gasps of wanting rose at once, and when his hand touched the moist portal, her torso leaped upward and she gave a sharp scream of delight.

"Yes, yes, yes . . . oh, jeez, yes," she cried as her hands clutched at him, once again moving frantically across his body as though she could somehow press him into her. When he rose and brought himself to her waiting warm wetness, she screamed. He slid forward slowly as she bucked and thrust and twisted, and once again he watched the small, firm breasts bounce as her entire body shuddered and leaped. A frenzied wildness seized her as he moved deeper, her legs slapping against him, her cries short, staccato screams of utter pleasure, her slender body lifting, bending, pushing, all of her around and against him, arms, legs, breasts in a frantic explosion, ecstasy gone berserk. "Yes, yes, yes, yes," she screamed, and suddenly her skin was wet, slipping against him, and he felt her trembling grow wilder, her head tossing from side to side, her fingers raking along his back. There was no stemming her scorching passion, and he felt himself swept along with the wildness that was hers, plunging harder and deeper and faster with her every urging.

Her screams grew louder, and he could feel the crescendo of ecstasy sweeping through her, the sweet contractions that clasped him. Then, with a suddenness that was not really sudden, her scream rose, tore from her, a cry of triumph and despair, of too much and not enough. It spiraled upward as her hands dug into shoulders, her teeth biting into his chest. The scream lingered in the air, her body refusing to surrender to the passing of ecstasy, the senses trying to hold what could not be held. When the last of the long scream died away, her body remained hard against him, clinging with desperation, every muscle tensed. Slowly, she relaxed, a deep cry coming from her as she fell back with her arms still around his neck, breasts still pressed against his chest. "Stay," she whispered, "stay." He obeyed, enjoying the warm wetness of her around him, the little contractions that still came until, finally, with a long, sighing sound, she lay still against him.

He took in her slender, piquant beauty, the little-gem body, each part perfectly wedded to each other part. His hands gently moved up and down her, heat still in her flesh. She turned, brought one thigh half over him, and pressed one small breast into his palm. Her blue eyes studied his face. "I surprised you," she said matter-of-factly.

"Yes," he admitted. "How'd you know?"

"I surprised myself," she said.

"You're a lot of explosion for a small package," he said.

"So's a stick of dynamite," she returned.

He conceded the reply with a laugh. "You've definitely been up here with your plants and seeds and notebooks for too long."

"Probably, but it wasn't just that. I tend to extremes. I can be very happy and very sad. I can get very angry, and I can be very determined and very lazy. I never forget a wrong or a right," she said. "Extremes, in work and in play."

"And in bed," he added, and she allowed a small, almost smug little smile to edge her lips. She lay back, her small breasts thrusting upward, her slender body beautifully molded, delicate yet with a quiet strength in its contours. Child-woman, he murmured silently, contrasts combining to make their own statement. When she half turned, her arms reached up and circled his neck. She brought the tiny nipples against his face, then slid downward teasingly.

"I won't be so frantic next time," she said.

"Don't buy that," he said and smiled.

"Why not?" She frowned.

"What's part of you stays part of you. It doesn't change, and it shouldn't," he said.

"You could be wrong about that," Linda said.

"There's a lot left of the night. Prove it," he said. She turned, half over him, and her mouth came to his at once, stayed, pressed, her tongue sliding forward with a delicious touch and quick movements. Only a few moments passed when he felt small shudders start to course through her, then her hands fluttering up and down his body. In a few more moments she was moving up and down against him, firm round, little rear lifting, then her pubic mound coming down atop him. He responded and felt her gathering her own momentum, short gasped cries in rhythm with

36

her every motion. He almost smiled as he wondered if one can measure frenzy—or the explosion of passion, the depth of pleasure. Did it matter? he asked inwardly. No, he decided as he rose to match her wildness, and once again the night echoed with her half screams and cries of absolute delight.

When the darkness rang with her final cries, she clung to him until the last shuddered remnant of passion came to an end. She lay still, hard against him, one small breast against his lips. "You win," he heard her whisper. He smiled and looked down to find she had already fallen into a deep sleep. He closed his eyes and slept with her wrapped around him, to wake only when the sound of the morning songbirds heralded the new day.

He slid from her, then paused to enjoy the sight of her for a long moment. Lying still and naked, she was a little girl again, upturned, pointed breasts delicately curved, slender body, all of her looking deceptively immature. Contrasts, he thought, a combination of contrasts. Pushing himself from the bed, he washed and was dressed when she woke, sat up, and drew the sheet around herself. "Little late for modesty," he commented.

"Not modesty," she said, almost with annoyance.

"What then?" he questioned.

"Last night was last night," she said.

"Keeping things separate?" he asked.

"Always." She shrugged.

"I'll use your wagon while you're dressing. Want to clean up some leftovers," he said, and she nodded as he walked from the house. He went around to the back, hitched the gray mare to the huckster wagon, and walked to where the two bodies lay beside the smaller cabin. He searched both, looking for badges, anything that might identify them, but found nothing. Tossing them into the wagon, he drove on, then found the other two men and searched them before putting them into the wagon. He drove on until he found a narrow, deep ravine that plunged down to a bottom he couldn't see.

He tossed the four of them into the ravine, grimly remembering that they had been prepared to kill him and Linda. He drove the wagon slowly back up the winding road and paused to survey the lush, dense greenery of the Appalachians. Their towering, forbidding beauty reached out, enveloping with its deep, dark fastness. They spoke in their own silent way, called out to all who dared intrude on their domain. This is the beginning place, they said, the first place, the first challenge of the New World. No empty boast but a truth as towering as their majestic peaks. This was the home of those first pioneers, those original settlers who landed on the shores of the place now called Virginia. The Appalachians were the first of the New World's towering obstacles after the first settlers landed in Jamestown in 1607.

Fargo's thoughts went to the great Western plains he had crossed and crisscrossed so often. The new battles, new hardships, and new sacrifices were all being fought there in the wild, untamed lands of the West, but in truth they were all echoes. Every wagon train that rolled along the Oregon, Santa Fe, Gila River, and Mormon trail was an echo of those who had crossed the Appalachians. Every fierce Cheyenne, Crow, Sioux, and Comanche attack was an echo of the attacks by the Delaware, Susquehannock, and Virginia Algonquians. The terrible Plains winters and their deadly famines followed the agony of the Jamestown settlers during the "starving time" when five hundred came and only sixty survived.

This land and these Appalachians were indeed a seed place for brutal massacres, famine, hardships, and perseverance. Here is where the seeds took root despite everything for the new nation, for the growth pains and the killing that was still going on across the untamed and unexplored western territories. This was the cradle place where those first settlers left their legacy, the land that held the first blood of a dream still being formed.

Now, in the two hundred and some years since those first settlers landed in Jamestown, dogged determination and new ideals, mind and muscle, faith and ambition had all combined to transform the land into a civilized place of laws and manners. Virginia shouldered the very heart of the government of the Untied States in Washington. Kentucky, Delaware, Maryland, North and South Carolina, Alabama, all bound by geography and spirit, had become part of this new civilized transformation. All the pursuits of civilized countries flourished—art, architecture, literature, government, business, everything to rival much of Europe. But with everything glamorous in this new society, the unglamorous and the undesirable also came, flourishing too well, legacies brought to these new shores that became a sickness, devouring the fabric of society as surely as the boll weevil ate away at the cotton.

But despite a society still growing, spreading westward, the deep Appalachians stayed inviolate, their depths and their secrets, their primordial strengths a constant reminder of the supreme power of nature. Explorers made their way through the green, towering mountains, found ways for others to follow, but their tracks were loose threads on a vast carpet, quickly absorbed and wiped away. The Appalachians ruled their green depths from the Blue Ridge Mountains to the Alleghenies to the Shenandoah Valley. Man was a trespasser, sometimes tolerated, more often destroyed. But the Appalachians stayed, a towering line that stretched between and separated the new civilization from the beckoning regions beyond. They remained apart from the growing country, an unconquered symbol of the great unconquered mountains that lay in the untamed West. They, too, were part of this first place, this cradle land.

He shook aside his thoughts and moved the wagon forward. Linda was waiting when he reached her place. She wore black Levi's and a white cotton blouse, dark blond hair brushed and hanging full around her face. "I'm ready to go," she said. He gave her the reins and brought his horse around, tying the Ovaro behind the wagon. She cast a glance at him as he slid onto the seat beside her. "Thought you might stay on," she commented, an edge of reproach in her voice.

"I've a man to meet," he said.

"Maybe you'll come back."

"I'd like that," he said, and she snapped the reins over the gray mare.

"I'll be here taking care of Kenny for a while, I'd guess," Linda said. "In a way it'll be like old times for me. After Mother died, I raised him," nostalgia coming into her voice as she reminisced. Then her face tightened. "He's going to tell me what he's got himself into. I'm going to insist on that," she said. Fargo let her go on, unwilling to dispel the optimism he couldn't share. When the hollow at the base of the mountain came into view, he saw Doc Benton waiting outside. He read the man's face at once and grimaced inwardly as Linda halted and swung from the wagon.

"Glad you're here," the mountain doctor said. "He's conscious at the moment, but he can't really talk. Too much of his throat's been destroyed." Linda brushed past him as she hurried into the house, and Fargo followed, slowing beside the doctor to stand back as Linda stopped at the bedside, bent over the figure of her brother wrapped in sheets.

"Kenny, it's me. I'm here. Can you hear me?" she asked. "Kenny, it's Linda." There was a flutter of Kenny Corrigan's eyes. "Yes, yes . . . good," Linda murmured encouragingly. The young man's eyelids opened, and he stared at Linda. Fargo saw slow recognition come into his face, and Kenny's lips moved soundlessly. "Easy, Kenny, easy," Linda said soothingly.

Fargo's voice was a whisper only Doc Benton could hear. "Can he talk?"

The doctor's head moved from side to side. "Every attempt tears away at what little is left of his vocal cords," he whispered back.

"Will he make it?" Fargo asked.

Doc Benton gave a helpless shrug. "He's lost too much blood. I'm surprised he's still alive."

Fargo saw Kenny Corrigan's lips work again. A hollow, whistling sound fought through his lips, a hoarse rasp. "He's trying to tell me something." Linda threw an agonized glance back at the doctor. "Can't you give him something? Water, maybe?"

"No, that won't help," the doctor said, and Linda turned back to her brother.

"Don't try to talk. Just rest," she said. But Kenny, perhaps aware that time was near an end for him, moved his lips again. A terrible sound came from his mouth, air being forced through the remnants of his throat, and Fargo saw the strain in the neck muscles that bulged.

"Dub . . . dub," he managed with the strained, hollow sound. Fargo stepped closer and leaned forward. "Dub," Kenny Corrigan rasped again, each effort showing excruciating pain in his face. Again, with his eyes fluttering, Kenny managed a sound. "L," he croaked. "L. Dub. L." The sounds came, each a tremendous effort, each fashioned of a coarse, whistling rasp.

"What is it, Kenny? What are you trying to say?" Linda cried, despair in her voice. But Kenny emitted only a low, hollow whistling noise now as, his eyes half open, he stared at the ceiling.

Fargo turned over the sounds Kenny had made in his mind, repeated them to himself as Linda looked at him with helpless despair. "Dub. L. Dub," Fargo muttered. "Dub. L. He's trying to say double." Fargo felt excitement rush into his own voice. Linda turned from him and leaned over her brother.

"Why, Kenny, why? Who did this?" she asked.

Fargo's eyes stayed on Kenny Corrigan, saw his lips draw back, and then a shuddering, croaking hollow whistle came from the youth's throat, truly a death rattle. The sound hung in the air, and then there was only silence, the final silence of death. Linda's anguished cry broke the hush as she flung herself across the still form, her sobs coming in deep gasps. Fargo stepped back and moved from the room to the open doorway as Linda's sobs filled the house. He was outside when she finally grew still and came out with Doc Benton holding her arm.

"I'll take care of everything," the doctor said.

"I'll come back after I get my things. I'll be driving him to the family plot outside of Fredericksburg," Linda said to the doctor.

"Everything will be ready," Doc Benton said and went back inside the house. Linda halted beside Fargo. Her eyes were still moist, but the muscles of her jaw throbbed with rage, he saw.

"I'm going to find out who did this, who's responsible," Linda said through clenched teeth. "That's a promise you can count on."

"I'm sorry about how it turned out," Fargo said.

Her nod acknowledged his condolences, but her eyes remained ice blue. She had let rage push aside grief, he saw. "What was he trying to tell me? What did he mean by the word *double*?" she asked. "Was he trying to say double back? Was he trying to warn me that those men might double back, looking for him? He'd no way of knowing they'd already done that."

"Double back," Fargo echoed, thinking aloud. "Maybe that's what he was trying to say, and maybe it was something else. Maybe he was trying to say double-edged, a warning to you about something that might have two sides. Or maybe he wanted to say double talk, a warning about someone who might come see you."

"Maybe he wanted to say double deal or double cross. Maybe he was trying to tell me he'd been lied to, deceived," Linda said, taking up his speculation.

"I'm afraid we'll never know," Fargo said.

"I'll know. I'll find out. I won't stop till I do," Linda said, determination surging through her voice. "Right now I've got to put things in order at the house before I leave."

"I'll give you a hand," he said.

"Thanks. It'll go faster with help," she said, and he climbed onto the seat beside her. She drove fast, wrapped in the silence of her own thoughts, but he saw the grief mixed with anger in the tightness of her face. When they reached the house, she swung to the ground and immediately began covering the rows of clay pots with small squares of canvas. "You can take the watering can and spray the plants in the wooden boxes against the side wall," she said.

He found the can and the small well, then began wetting down the growths in each of the long boxes. "Seems you're not figuring to come back here after the burial," he said.

"That's right. I'm going to visit the man Kenny told me he was working for," Linda said, ice in her voice.

"Kenny never told you what kind of work it was?" Fargo questioned.

"No. I asked, but he wouldn't talk about it, said it was very secret. He implied it had to do with the government. He told me it often took him to Washington," Linda said. "I hated hearing that. I know the government."

"Meaning what?" Fargo asked.

"They don't keep their word, and they use people, especially young, idealistic people like Kenny. That's why Mister Ben Stott is going to be my first stop," Linda said, tightening the last piece of canvas.

Fargo felt his mouth fall open. "Who?" he asked, blurting out the word.

"Ben Stott, the man Kenny worked for," Linda answered.

Fargo stared at her as the note in his jacket pocket suddenly seemed to vibrate. "You sure that's the name?" he queried.

"Of course I'm sure. He's got a place up from Chancellorsville. Why?" She frowned.

"Ben Stott is the man I'm going to meet," Fargo said slowly, and Linda straightened, stared back at him. "Hard Rock Road, alongside the Rapidan River."

"That's right." Linda nodded. "He's the man who wants you to break a new trail for him through the Appalachians?"

"Yes. I don't fancy there could be two Ben Stotts, both at the same address," Fargo said.

"Not likely," Linda agreed. "I'm sure he's one and the same. This means we can go visit him together."

"Guess so," Fargo said, still thinking about the coincidence of it.

"Only I get to talk to him first," Linda said.

"That's fine with me." Fargo finished his watering as Linda hurried into the house. The frown stayed on his brow. Coincidences happened. He'd seen enough of them to know that. But what was Kenny Corrigan doing for a man who wanted a new trail broken? Why had Kenny hinted to Linda that he was involved in some secret government work? To impress his big sister? Young men had done exactly that sort of thing often enough. But that explanation shredded when he thought about the four killers. They were all too real, and they had killed Kenny. Why? Did they fit in with Ben Stott? How did four killers fit in with a man who wanted a new trail broken? Did they fit in at all, or was Kenny Corrigan into something all on his own? The questions continued to tumble over one another in his mind. Nothing was simple anymore.

Ben Stott had questions to answer. Fargo knew Linda would demand answers. She came from the house with two canvas traveling bags that Fargo helped put into the wagon. "I'm ready," she said, took the reins, and he slid in beside her. When they reached Pine Hollow, the doctor had the simple pine box sealed shut. Fargo helped him put it into the wagon, where he just was able to close the tailboard. "Good journey," Doc Benton said as Linda rolled the wagon forward, Fargo's pinto trotting along behind.

She drove in silence. She knew her way out of the mountains, and soon they were rolling across a land of gentle hills and long, flat stretches that grew thick with rich bluegrass and a profusion of wildflowers. This land was not manicured, yet it held an orderliness where red mulberry shouldered white ash and honey locust grew alongside hawthorn and hemlock, and they all were neat companions. Yet he saw plenty of sudden wild places with ravines and cuts and rapidly flowing waterways. Large Virginia plantations soon appeared, stretched out for acres and acres to disappear when the land grew wild again. A country of mixtures, this Virginia, Fargo decided, not unlike Linda Corrigan. He idly took mental notes as Linda left the roads, took shortcuts, and arrived at a small cemetery when the sun was still young. Two men came from a caretaker's house, and she stepped from the wagon to meet them. They spoke briefly. They took the pine box, and Linda unhitched the wagon, flung a saddle on the gray mare, and rode to where Fargo waited.

"Let's go," she said impatiently. He knew the impatience was only part of anguish. He was sorry there was little he could do to help her with that pain. But then, he wasn't sure she really wanted help. Grief could be cathartic, especially for some people, and she was one of them.

"How long a ride now?" he asked as they moved on.

"We should get to Ben Stott before the day's end," she said, and rode alongside him, letting silence be a kind of neutral territory between them. They reached the shores of the Rapidan when Fargo pointed to a road that wound its way beside the narrow river.

"That looks like it's the road we want," he said, and she followed as he swung onto the round, rutted roadway.

"I'll speak my piece. You speak yours," Linda said.

"Wouldn't have it any other way," he answered, and they rode perhaps another mile when the house came into sight. He frowned at a square, unattractive, unpainted structure. Two horses were tied at the rear of the house under a three-sided lean-to, along with a single-seat buckboard. He halted and slid from the saddle as Linda drew to a halt and climbed down.

A man came from the house, a lean, spare figure, balding, clothed in white shirt, red suspenders, and loose trousers. He wore a gun belt that held a heavy Remington six-shot single-action pistol. Fargo took in watery blue eyes set far apart that made a thin nose seem even thinner, a face that managed to be both bland and wary. Linda stepped forward briskly. "Ben Stott?" she asked.

"That's right," the man answered. His eyes went to Fargo. "You two together?" he asked.

"Yes and no," Fargo said, and Ben Stott frowned. "We met, found out we were both on the way to see you, and decided to come together. I'm Fargo."

The man's eyes widened at once. "Fargo. Been waiting for you," he said, growing more animated.

"I'm Linda Corrigan," Linda cut in, and Ben Stott turned to her, no expression in his face. "Kenny Corrigan's sister," Linda said, and Ben Stott allowed faint acknowledgment to cross his face. "Kenny's dead," Linda said. This time Ben Stott's carefully bland expression cracked.

"Let's go inside," he said, and turned to the house. Linda followed, and Fargo stepped along behind her. He halted in a large almost furnitureless entranceway to another room that held a desk and chairs and little else.

"I'll wait out here," Fargo said. Linda beckoned for him to come with her, but he stayed, and she went into the next room. She left the door half open, and he could see Ben Stott move behind the desk.

"That's terrible news," the man said to Linda. "An accident?"

"A murder," Linda snapped, and Ben Stott's face stayed expressionless. "Four men hunted him down and killed him."

Ben Stott let shock cross his face. "My God. Highwaymen, of course. It happens all the time, unfortunately."

"No highwaymen," Linda said flatly. "Killers who were out after Kenny. I want to know why. I thought you might have an idea."

"I can't think of anyone with a reason to kill Kenny," the man said.

"What was he doing for you?" Linda questioned.

"I keep records, deeds and claims, family statistics, livestock records, land records, that sort of thing. I hired Kenny to assist me," the man said.

"Kenny told me his job was secret and often took him to Washington," Linda said.

Ben Stott offered a tolerant smile. "I'm afraid Kenny had an active imagination," he said calmly.

"He didn't imagine his killers," Linda snapped. "They were very real, and they hunted him down. I want to know why."

Ben Stott shrugged. "Maybe they were the kind that enjoyed killing. There are plenty of those around."

"No. They came after me, too. They wanted to make sure Kenny was dead. Fargo was there. He'll verify it," Linda said.

"You ever think that Kenny might have had personal enemies, young lady?" Ben Stott asked, still keeping his voice tolerant.

"Kenny wasn't into gambling or anything like that. I'm convinced this has something to do with his work for you. Why did it bring him to Washington so often?" Linda pressed.

"It didn't," Ben Stott said, his tolerant demeanor suddenly disappearing. "I've told you what little I know. I've nothing else to say."

"I don't believe you," Linda said, and Fargo saw the man's face harden.

"That's your privilege. My condolences again, and this conversation is over. Good day," Ben Stott said brusquely.

"My finding out the truth sure as hell isn't over," Linda threw back, spun on her heel, and strode from the room. She passed Fargo, her quick glance one of barely contained fury.

"Fargo," Ben Stott called, and Fargo stepped into the room. "Please close the door and sit down," the man said. Fargo pushed the door shut and lowered himself into a straight-backed chair. "That young woman is very upset. I'm sorry for her," Ben Stott said.

"She's got reason," Fargo said. "They hunted down her brother and then came after her."

"Are you saying that you share in Miss Corrigan's imaginings?" the man asked carefully.

"I'm saying I'd have questions if I were in her place, and I'm stacking up my own questions," Fargo said.

The man's lips pursed. "I suppose that's to be expected, things coming together as they did." He paused, and Fargo waited silently. "I can clear up a few things," Ben Stott continued. "You were not asked to come here to break a new cattle trail. That's the word we put out. After all, you are the Trailsman. Your reputation is widely known. It seemed the most plausible reason."

"Who is *we*?" Fargo asked.

"You'll find out in time," Ben Stott said.

"Why'd you send for me, the real reason?" Fargo questioned.

"You'll be told that in time," the man said.

"When?" Fargo pressed.

"When you get to Washington," Stott replied.

Fargo's brows rose. "Washington?" he echoed. "What's this all about? Why the secrecy?"

"The secrecy is because there are spies, informants, secret operatives, and hired killers everywhere. This is a time of turmoil and danger, though you're not aware of that yet. Most people aren't, but it's true. That's why we transmit information in small doses so no one, except those at the very top, can be made to reveal more than a piece of anything."

"Informants, hired killers, like the ones who did in Kenny Corrigan?"

"Probably," Ben Stott allowed.

"How do you fit into this?" Fargo asked, staring hard at the man.

"I am an agent of the government, your government," Stott said.

"I'm thinking that Linda Corrigan's not wrong in what she suspects." Fargo frowned.

"Forget about Linda Corrigan and her suspicions," the man said.

"Give me a good reason. Start leveling with me," Fargo shot back.

Ben Stott paused. "I can tell you this much. You've been called here to do a vital service for your country. You'll learn how vital when you get to Washington.

Perhaps the very future of the country depends on what you can do, Fargo."

"Those are mighty big words," Fargo said.

"And I've chosen them carefully," Ben Stott answered.

Fargo peered hard at the man and decided Ben Stott believed what he'd said. The words hung in the air, words a man couldn't lightly turn aside. But he wasn't at all satisfied. "You brought me here with a lie. Give me something to cut the taste of it, something to make me believe those big words," he challenged.

Ben Stott's lips pursed as he turned over thoughts before answering. "If I can't? Or don't? What happens?" he asked.

"I'll be heading back to the prairie."

"You drive a hard bargain, Fargo."

"I don't like a crooked trail," Fargo said.

3

"What if I tell you what I can about Kenny Corrigan?" Ben Stott offered.

"That'd help. It'd be a start," Fargo said.

Ben Stott grimaced, looking unhappy as he began to answer. "Kenny worked for me as a courier, and yes, he often went to Washington, sometimes twice a week. He was good, but he had access to a lot of very secret and important information."

"You saying that's what got him killed?" Fargo frowned.

"Could be. Or he found out something and had to be silenced," Stott said.

"Why didn't he come to you with whatever he found out?" Fargo questioned.

"Probably because he thought they'd be waiting for him if he tried to reach my place. I suspect he thought he'd be safe hiding out in the mountains at his sister's place," Ben Stott said.

"He was wrong," Fargo said grimly.

"They were probably already on his tail," Stott said.

"Who?" Fargo questioned.

The man thought for a moment. "Could have been a lot of people. I'll let Washington fill you in on that."

"Why didn't you level with Linda?" Fargo pressed.

"This is inside information. I only told you because you pressured me into it. I don't want her poking around. She could do more harm than good. She's also an unknown quantity. We don't know anything about her attitudes, her politics, her thoughts, her sympathies, her friends. We don't trust unknown quantities. You can't, either. You'd best remember that."

Fargo stared at the man. "I'm thinking you don't trust many people," he said.

The faintest of smiles touched Ben Stott's lips. "That's a fair enough statement," he admitted.

"You trusted Kenny Corrigan."

"I hope I was right," the man said.

"What's that mean?" Fargo queried.

"It means a man can be killed for what he's found out, for keeping a trust, or for betraying somebody. I'll know where Kenny Corrigan fits in after we know who killed him," Ben Stott said. "The very fact that he was hunted down and killed makes him a question mark."

"That's pretty damn callous," Fargo said.

"This is a callous time," Stott said. "Now I'll give you your instructions. You go to Washington, the Hotel Plymouth. You'll wait there for a Mister John Nicolay. He'll fill you in on his role. A day after your meeting with John Nicolay there'll be a fancy formal ball and dinner at the home of Cornelia Jeffers. Cornelia is a well-known Washington hostess. Nicolay will be there. You're to meet him there. He'll give you further instructions."

"I'm not happy with any of this. It's still a crooked trail, and I'm riding in the dark," Fargo said.

"That'll end soon," Ben Stott said. "A last reminder. Linda Corrigan's not to know any of this. Send her packing."

"That might not be so easy. She's got a lot of bull-dog in her."

"Send her back to her plants and the mountains. You'll be doing her a favor. The less she pokes around, the safer she'll be."

"From who?" Fargo grunted, but received no reply. "Will I be hearing from you again?" he asked.

"It's possible, but probably not," the man said. "You're going to be proud of what you'll be doing."

"I hope so," Fargo muttered as he walked from the room and strode into the late afternoon. He had reached the Ovaro when Linda came over to him, her dark blue eyes searching his face.

"You have a nice talk with Ben Stott?" she asked.

"Nice enough. We talked about the kind of trail he wants me to find for him," Fargo said.

Linda fastened a skeptical stare at him. "That all?" she asked.

"That's right."

"Nothing about me or Kenny?" she pressed.

"We had our own business to talk about," Fargo said and felt traitorous as he watched her adjust the bit chain on the mare.

"You going to work for him?" she asked carefully.

"No reason not to," Fargo said.

"That's a matter of opinion," she said tartly.

He ignored the comment. "You'll be going back to your place, I take it."

"Wrong," she said, snapping out the word. "He lied to me about everything."

"You really think that?" Fargo asked blandly.

"I know it, and I'm going to find out the truth," Linda said.

Fargo chose his words carefully. "Maybe you ought to back off."

"Why?" She frowned.

He shrugged and scrambled to find a good reason. "Maybe you won't like what you find out," he said.

"I'm not afraid of that. Kenny was clean," she said with no hesitation. "Somebody killed him. I'm going to find out who's responsible."

"Some things are best left alone."

"This isn't one of them," she threw back.

"Why risk your neck? It'll come out in time," he said.

"A lot of things never come out. I can't depend on that, and I'm not going to," she said and held him with a sidelong glance. "Ben Stott would have had better excuses for me," she said.

"I was thinking about you," he said, knowing he sounded hurt. It helped cover up feeling guilty, he thought.

She softened. "Thanks," she said. Then her eyes widened as he swung onto the Ovaro. "You going?"

she asked, and he nodded. "I'm surprised," she said, suddenly cool again. "I thought we might have the night. I expected you'd want to repeat the other night as much as I. My mistake."

"Time's grown more important," he said and cursed silently. "There's enough day left for me to use. I've got to use it."

"By all means. Don't let me stop you," she said icily.

"I'd like to stop back when this is all over," he said, trying to soothe her hurt.

"Anytime," she said, but her tone meant exactly the opposite.

Her eyes stayed on him as he moved the Ovaro forward. She didn't return his wave, and he swore silently as he rode on. Maybe she'd think about the things he said, but she'd not change her mind. There was too much bitter anger in her for that.

Putting the pinto into a trot, he rode north for a few miles before he turned east and rode across easy-to-travel terrain, the land mostly flat and dotted with forest growths. He'd not make Washington for another day, he realized, and didn't push the horse. When the sun began to lower, he came to a large forest of American sycamore. He cast a glance behind him as he rode past the forest, a gesture born of habit, second nature to him now. His eyes automatically scanned the tall green walls of the forest and watched a flock of Baltimore orioles take flight from the center of the trees in an explosion of black and orange. A small, errant breeze caressed the tops of the trees and moved the leaves undulatingly.

His gaze moved downward, halting as he spied the trees where the low branches moved in a straight line. A frown instantly on his brow, he moved the horse forward another hundred yards, drew to a halt, and slid from the saddle. Only one thing caused the exact motion pattern, and he decided to be certain. He bent down, ostensibly examining the pinto's left pastern. Keeping his head down, he peered out from under the brim of his hat. The low branches were still, and he uttered a grim snort. He'd proved the movement. He was being followed, and the follower had halted as he did. Fargo straightened up, returned to the saddle, and rode on. Ben Stott's words came to him. *There are spies, informants, secret operatives, and hired killers everywhere. This is a time of turmoil and danger.*

He continued to ride casually, his jaw tight, and as the sun lowered, he turned the Ovaro into the edge of the sycamores before dusk became dark. He reined to a halt, kept the saddle on the horse, took down his saddlebag, and stretched out under the trees. He waited: the moon came up enough to filter its paleness through the canopy of sycamores. He rose, then took a stick of dried beef from the saddlebag and ate, washed it down with water from his canteen. When he finished, he lay back, his eyes half shut but his ears straining to pierce the night. Finally, he rose again and on the balls of his feet moved through the trees. He moved carefully, each step silent as the tread of a lynx. As he walked, he drew the night air into his nostrils, smelled the dampness of it, and let his nose become his eyes and ears.

He moved left, then right, then left again, each step a silent, careful motion, when he suddenly halted. His nostrils flared, and he drew in the odor of leather and horse. Moving forward again, he followed his nose, halting beside a sapling as he discerned the figure curled on a blanket. He drew the Colt as he started closer, then halted again as the figure took shape, and he saw short, dark blond hair and a smallish figure fully clothed. He straightened, keeping the Colt in his hand. "I'll be dammed," he said aloud. The form bolted up, eyes snapping open, focusing on him. He kept the Colt aimed. "I most always know when I'm being followed," he said quietly.

Linda Corrigan swallowed, pushed herself to her feet, and eyed the Colt. "You can put that down," she said.

"When I'm ready," he grunted. "Why?" he asked, his voice hardening.

"It seems Ben Stott isn't the only one who lied to me," she said.

"How'd you know?" he asked.

"All the time you were talking to me you were uncomfortable," Linda said. "You're not the only one who can read signs."

"Guess not," he conceded and dropped the Colt into its holster.

"There was something else," she said with a touch of smugness.

"What?"

"I couldn't believe you'd turn away from another night like last night just to make up some time. There had to be another reason. Call it conceit, wisdom, whatever you like," she said. He uttered a wry sound at the acumen of the female. "Seems I was right," she added.

"I didn't lie, not exactly," he said.

"Exactly enough," she snapped back. She didn't allow any concessions, he saw, and found a grudging admiration for her.

"Get your horse. You might as well bed down with me," he said. She took the mare by the cheekstrap and followed him to where he'd left the Ovaro. She sat down near him as he lay on the carpet of bluegrass.

"You want to start telling the truth?" she asked.

Ben Stott's warnings came back to him once again. *She's an unknown quantity. We don't trust unknown quantities. You can't, either.* His eyes moved over Linda's pleasant face. She wasn't completely unknown to him, not anymore. She was a passionate young woman, a combination of contrasts, scientist-botanist and anxious little girl. But that's all he knew about her, he realized. She was an unknown quantity in every other respect. Ben Stott was right about that.

But it was not the man's cynical warning that stayed. He didn't know very much himself, but he'd become convinced that telling Linda what little he knew wouldn't help her. It could more likely push her into very real danger. Ben Stott's words swam into his mind again. *The less she pokes around the safer she'll be.*

Linda's voice broke into his racing thoughts. "I'm waiting," she hissed.

"Don't have anything to tell you," he said.

"More lies," she threw back. "You're not going back to the Appalachians to break trail. You're riding in the opposite direction."

"I'll be going back. I'm meeting a man with more instructions," he said, the answer not really a lie.

Her eyes speared into him. "You're heading northeast. I'd say you're on your way to Washington," she said.

He swore silently. "Now, what makes you think that?" Fargo asked, tolerant amusement in his tone.

"Am I wrong?" she countered confidently.

"Lucky guess," he admitted.

"No. Washington plays a part in what happened to Kenny. Ben Stott sent him there often enough. Now you're heading that way," Linda said.

He clung to his half-amused smile. "All right, I'm going to meet somebody there, that's all. Nothing mysterious. All very ordinary," he said.

"So ordinary you couldn't tell me," Linda snapped pointedly.

He swore again under his breath. She was too sharp for games. "Let's put it this way. I'm as much in the dark as you are," he tried.

"Obviously not," she interrupted.

"More than you think," he said. "But I do know this is no time for amateurs. You could lose your life. Go back to your work. Do yourself a favor."

"And just forget about Kenny? No. I want the truth,

here and now, not in some story years away. I want those responsible to pay," she said. "I thought you might help me, but I see I was wrong."

"Dammit, I can't help you till I know more myself. You'll have to wait. Meanwhile, you go poking around, you could get yourself killed," he said angrily.

"It's plain you know more than you're telling me," Linda said.

"Not enough to help you," he insisted.

She peered at him. "I don't hear any promises."

"Promises?" He frowned.

"To tell me what you do find out," she challenged.

His lips tightened. She was good at backing someone into a corner. But she failed to realize that ploy could stiffen backs more than loosen tongues. "No promises, not till I know more," he told her.

"I'm sorry for that," she said.

"Me, too," he said, and she lay back on the blanket, her upturned breasts pointing to the tree canopy. "Linda," he murmured softly, "the night's still young enough."

She pushed up on one elbow. "Passion's all right, but not promises? Like Hell, Skye Fargo, like hell."

"You wanted tonight. You still do."

"That's right," she admitted. "But the answer is still no. Surprised?"

He studied her for a moment. "No. Disappointed," he said.

"Good," she sniffed, turned her back to him, and curled up on the blanket. He pulled off most of his clothes and drew sleep around himself until morning came. He woke and saw Linda lying in slender loveliness, her arms hiding the saucy breasts. He rose and found a small stream and was through washing and dressed when Linda appeared. She wore a skirt, but shed it at the stream, and he watched her slender beauty and thought of the wild, passion-driven figure that had been atop him. He was saddling the Ovaro when she reappeared, clothed in a fresh shirt and the black skirt. "I'll ride along for a spell. I'm going in the same direction," she said. "If you're not minding," she added with a touch of sarcasm.

"Glad for the company," he said. After breakfasting on pine nuts and wild cherries, she rode beside him as he traveled the rolling countryside, passing one plantation after another. The morning had drifted into early afternoon when they crossed the Bull Run, and he was happy to have Linda show him the best spot to cross. Wagon traffic increased as they drew closer to Alexandria and Arlington, and he skirted smaller communities as he neared Washington. She rode with him and made no attempt to talk of promises and justice and vengeance. He gave her credit for that.

In sight of Washington the buildings rose in the distance, the roads smoother, the houses well tended. She slowed and pointed to a large house at the end of a tree-lined road. He took in architecture that seemed modified colonial, a house not imposing, yet not modest.

"The family home," Linda said. "I guess it's all mine now. My father lived here for many years after Mother died. He was a teacher of botany."

"You followed in his footsteps."

"Yes. He used to take me to all the creeks that flow behind the house. Fishing was one of his loves. Hunting was another. He'd go into the Shenandoah Valley for that, deep into the mountains. He hunted quail, grouse, wild turkey, pine squirrels, and bear. He'd camp in the Shenandoah a week or two each trip. I didn't go with him all the time, but often enough." She halted abruptly, her nostalgia snapped off almost angrily. "We were a solid family," she said. "I'll be leaving you now. Sorry it has to be like this."

"It doesn't have to be like this," he said. "Go back to your plants. I'll come by in time."

"I'm not backing off," Linda said, her voice hard. "Kenny was the last of the family, 'cept for me. Somebody's responsible for his death. Somebody's going to pay. I don't care where the chips fall."

"You've a vengeful streak, girl," Fargo said.

"You call it vengeful. I call it justice, and we sure as hell need more of that around here," Linda answered. She gestured toward the house. "Chantilly Road. Come visit if you ever get ready to help me."

"Maybe," he said. "I don't know what's waiting for me."

"Me neither," she said.

He leaned over and kissed her cheek. She didn't pull away, but she didn't respond either. A creature of extremes, she had called herself. It fitted. He left her, put the pinto into a trot, and didn't look back. She had already turned away, he was certain.

4

It was a moonless night, clouds curtaining the sky, when Her Majesty's ship *Aberdeen Clipper* lay four miles off the coast of Virginia, where the Chesapeake Bay joined the Atlantic. A British merchantman, the *Aberdeen Clipper* lay silent in the dark waters, almost invisible. Every light on her long, graceful deck was out, even the running lights. The only lamp lit was inside the captain's cabin at the stern, and that was shrouded behind the drawn curtains covering the latticed windows. Two small dories nestled against the sleek side of the vessel, and inside the captain's cabin five men sipped from a bottle of Pedro Domecq Oloroso.

The *Aberdeen Clipper* had been chosen for the secret meeting for a number of reasons. She was one of the first of the "iron clippers," a fleet built by the famous shipbuilders Jones, Quigg and Company of Liverpool, whose hulls were made of iron instead of wood. She was considered a reliable vessel, most likely to be at the appointed place at the appointed time. But even more important, American naval authorities knew the

Aberdeen Clipper as a regular trading visitor and would give it no special scrutiny. Even now its holds were filled with hemp, mother-of-pearl, gum, copal, railroad iron, and seven hundred of the finest York hams. Plus a safe with a quarter million dollars to pay for the cargo it expected to take back to England.

Senator John Slidell put down his glass of sherry, brushed back the white hair he parted straight down the middle of his head, and regarded the others with a nervous smile. "I apologize for the inconvenience of this meeting place, but you all know we cannot be seen together. Each of us would be compromised if we were. Then they'd like nothing better than to accuse us of conspiring."

"Damn right," the man next to him agreed and mouthed his cigar, emblematic of his vast tobacco holdings. William Yancey, businessman turned politician, knew the power of money better than any of the others.

"Let's start with your report, Mr. Yancey," John Slidell said.

"Our treasury is growing, but not fast enough. That damn blockade is hurting us. We have to break it for us to succeed," the man said. "We need more money, and we need it now. That's my report, dammit."

At Yancey's right Congressman James Murray Mason looked uncomfortable, John Slidell noted. But then Mason was one of those men who always looked slightly uncomfortable.

"We're hurting them," Senator Slidell said. "As Mr. Yancey put it, we have to hurt them more. Each of us has our own contacts to inform and lean upon. Each of us is part of this great venture." He turned to the man directly opposite him, a small, wiry, very dapper figure in a sharply pressed uniform. A strong head seemed a trifle large for his body, and a thick head of dark, slightly wavy hair was echoed by a full mustache below a long, straight nose. Brown eyes held a glint of arrogance. "I'm especially glad you could join us for the meeting, General," Senator Slidell said, his manner and tone deferential.

General Pierre Gustave Toutant Beauregard nodded, his tone on the edge of patronizing. "Mobility is the key to deploying my men. They are scattered about in small units of ten each. In an instant I can produce ten or two hundred. We can guard an individual or a wagon train."

"Reassuring, most reassuring, General," the senator said. "Your presence in our operation gives us a new dimension. Your resignation as superintendant of West Point gave inspiration to thousands."

General Beauregard allowed a modest nod. "It gave me freedom to act," he said.

"Tell me, General, did you take your Spanish barber and your valet?" Slidell asked.

"Of course. They've been with me so long they are like family." General Beauregard smiled as Slidell turned to the fifth man in the cabin, a tall, thin figure clothed in an expensive Savile Row suit.

"Now, we must hear from Her Majesty's representative," the senator said, again with his deferential manner.

Sir Harvey Chambers, member of Parliament and special envoy to the American continent, bestowed a nod on the others, his thin, austere face reflecting a dislike for the task his government had assigned him. "The position of Her Majesty's government hasn't changed. We support you. We want to continue to furnish the money you need. We have an interdependence. We need your cotton, wool, tobacco, and lumber. You need the money we'll pay to finance your cause," Sir Harvey said. "But everything depends on your getting our ships through. This blockade must not succeed."

"It won't, I assure you, Sir Harvey," Slidell said. "We'd like our support broadened, more countries trading with us, paying us more monies. How does the British government view the French position?"

"The French are waiting, sitting on the fence, their favorite position. They've sent a special emissary, that twit Prince Napoleon, to feel out any weakness in the federal government. Once they are convinced you are strong enough to prevail, they'll come in on your side, but only then."

"We'll try to convince them," the senator said.

Congressman James Murray Mason spoke up, his voice as glum as his face. "You're all convinced there'll be conflict," he said.

"Of course. Aren't you?" Slidell frowned.

"Yes, but I keep hoping it can be avoided," Mason said.

"Not any longer. Things have gone too far," Slidell said.

"Not everybody thinks so," the congressman muttered.

General Beauregard cut in, his tone still on the edge of patronizing. "Poor judgment, the inability to evaluate a situation, is a major problem. I've written letters on that very thing about General Anderson," he said.

"Bob Anderson's a Kentuckian. He's sympathetic to our cause," Senator Slidell said. "He's a believer in human property, in the words of the Richmond Clarion."

"That's a wonderful euphemism," Sir Harvey said dryly.

"Our people feel that General Anderson is going to come over to our side. That's why they're not bothered by his taking command of Fort Sumter. They feel he'll surrender the fort," Slidell said.

"I've heard that, and they're wrong. That's why it's so important to know the man, know what makes him tick. General Anderson's life is ruled by four things—devotion to duty, the Ten Commandments, the U.S. Constitution, and the Army manual. He can't go against those things, no matter where his sympathies lie. I'm trying to convince people of that."

"Which brings me to our last item," Slidell said. "They've brought in a very special man, called him in all the way from the Western territories. He's known as the Trailsman. He can find tracks not even the Sioux can find, read a trail like a mountain lion, see signs only a hawk can see. He can be the greatest threat to our operation, which depends on secrecy, as you know."

"Yes. If your operation is stopped, you'll never break the blockade. From what you say, that means stopping this Trailsman," the general said.

"Skye Fargo," Slidell grunted. "I've agents on him already, but I may be calling on you for help, General. I'm told he's very hard to bring down."

"My men are waiting. Just call," General Beauregard said, rose to his feet, and took the last sip of his sherry. "It'll be dawn in another hour. It's time we went our ways," he said.

"Yes," Slidell agreed, and the others, except for Sir Harvey, began to move toward the cabin door. The senator paused beside the Englishman. "We'll be getting reports to you through channels, Sir Harvey," Slidell said.

"I've my own channels," Chambers said coolly. "All Her Majesty's government really wants to know is that our ships can get through. See to that, and the rest will follow."

Senator Slidell nodded as he filed from the cabin behind Yancey, his voice low as he reached the deck. "I wonder if they'll ever stop treating us like colonies," he grumbled.

"I don't give a damn how they treat us so long as they keep buying cotton and tobacco," Yancey snapped. "Which means you damn well better break that blockade once and for all."

Senator Slidell nodded as he frowned and thought about a man called the Trailsman. He had difficulty believing that one man could be the threat he'd been made out to be. Ridiculous, he muttered to himself. The Trailsman would pose no real threat, not with the agents he had at his command, Slidell told himself.

5

Fargo enjoyed the way the land changed character as he rode north, the plantations growing larger, the houses more impressive, the roads in better condition. This was rich land, this Virginia, rich in soil, in grass, in crops, and in history. Yet as he passed the vast fields being worked under a hot sun, he realized again that it was not unlike looking at a beautiful painting that almost covered the terrible flaws in it. He turned down a wide road flanked by rows of honey locust with their red-brown, flat seed pods that hung in graceful spirals. As he drew closer to the capital, he passed a steady procession of light pony wagons, drop-front phaetons, ladies driving phaetons and surreys with a good number of buckboards mixed in.

When he reached Washington in the early night, lamplight fell on a full clarence as well as broughams, landaulettes, and panel-boot victorias. Platform spring grocery wagons appeared, as did a baker's wagon and a cut-under milk wagon with the driver standing. He slowed on the well-tended streets, then stopped near the Potomac, where a vendor stood beside his cart. "Hotel Plymouth," he said.

"Stay on this street. You'll see it on your left," the man said. Fargo followed the directions as the street widened, and he listened to the sound of the Ovaro's hooves on the cobblestones. He passed three young women swathed in organdy evening gowns, inside the long, graceful lines of a three-spring caleche. There was little question that he was in Washington, he told himself. It had been a long time since he'd ridden the streets of a major city, and he felt a little like a fish out of water. The large building stood at his left, and he drew up in front of the modest sign that announced HOTEL PLYMOUTH. Dismounting, he went into an imposing lobby where gas lamps burned against wood-paneled walls and an air of quiet graciousness emanated from the space.

"Single, please," he said to an elderly clerk at the desk who just managed not to be disapproving in his glance at the riding clothes he wore.

"Room three, ground floor, end of the hallway," the man said, and handed him a key.

"Want to stable my horse," Fargo said.

"Right behind the hotel," the clerk said, and Fargo returned outside, found the stable, and put the Ovaro in a small but clean stall. He paused at the desk when he returned to the hotel.

"I'm expecting a Mister John Nicolay," he told the clerk and walked to the end of the hallway, where he found a small but neat and clean room with a single bed, a stand for a washbasin, and a dresser. He let the small lamp stay dark and stretched out on the bed to wait for his visitor. Only some fifteen minutes passed when he heard the knock, swung long legs from the bed, and opened the door, his hand on the butt of the Colt at his side. Three men faced him, all wearing black slickers and black, wide-brimmed Stetsons. The tallest had a gaunt face and a thin pencil mustache. "You Fargo?" he asked.

"That's right," Fargo said.

"There's been a change in plans. Mister Nicolay sent us to bring you to him," the man said.

"I'll get my horse," Fargo said.

"Don't bother. We've a carriage outside," the man said, then stepped back for Fargo to pass. The trio followed as Fargo walked from the hotel into the night and saw a heavy coupe painted black with curtained windows. A fourth man sat on the driver's seat in front of the carriage body. Fargo paused, his eyes moving across the carriage, momentarily surprised at the poor condition of the vehicle. One of the oil lamps was broken, the wood split under the driver's seat, and he saw two deep gashes in the left rear wheel rim. The gaunt-faced man held the door open, Fargo entered the carriage, and the three men followed. Two sat on the seat with him, one on each side, the gaunt-faced man taking the small seat facing him.

The carriage moved away at once with one of the curtains parted just enough to let a little light into the interior. "Where's John Nicolay?" Fargo asked.

"Waiting for you," the man said.

"Why the change in plans?" Fargo queried.

"Don't know. We just follow orders," the man said.

Fargo felt uneasiness creeping through him. He was getting evasive, uncommunicative answers. Perhaps it didn't mean anything, yet the skin at the back of his neck was tingling. His sixth sense nudged at him. It was seldom wrong. "How far?" he asked.

"Not far. Nicolay's place," the man said.

"Across town?" Fargo pressed.

"More or less," the answer came. Fargo swore silently. The answers continued to be evasive. He considered reaching for the Colt, but the two men on each side held him almost immobile.

"Why the curtains?" he questioned.

"Guess Mister Nicolay's afraid somebody might take a shot at you," the gaunt-faced man said.

The answer was less evasive, yet still unsatisfying, and Fargo lay his head back against the seat, his eyes half closed in the almost blackness inside the carriage. He listened with the ears of a cougar, ears that picked out and separated every sound. He heard the hard hoofbeats on the cobblestones of the Washington streets, listened as the hardness changed character when the carriage moved onto paved streets. His brow furrowed when the hoofbeats suddenly grew duller as the horse moved onto hard-packed earth. They were on a road, a smooth, well-used road. Perhaps ten minutes more went by when he heard the hoofbeats change tone again, become a softer, thudding sound. No hard-packed roadbed now—he frowned—a soft, perhaps damp path. They had left the streets of Washington, that much was now clear.

Uneasiness became alarm. Something was very wrong. He started to gather himself when he felt a hard object pressed into his right side, then another push into his left ribs. He had no need to wonder what they were. He had felt the barrel of a six-gun too many times to mistake the feel of it. The gaunt-faced man leaned across the carriage, and Fargo stayed motionless as the Colt was pulled from his holster. The man sat back and dropped the Colt into a pocket in his slicker as thoughts tumbled through Fargo's mind. Maybe he could buy a little time, find a moment to make a move. "Who sent you?" he asked.

"The tooth fairy." The man laughed nastily.

"Where's John Nicolay?" Fargo questioned.

"Probably on his way to see you," the man said, and laughed again.

But his answer had cleared up one thing. Nicolay had no part in the attack. But somebody did. *There are spies, informants, secret operatives, and hired killers everywhere.* Ben Stott plainly knew what he was talking about. Fargo felt the carriage begin to jounce. They had left the path and rolled across uneven ground. The two guns stayed pressed into his ribs, and he cursed in silent frustration as the carriage slowly came to a halt. The driver swung down and pulled the door open, then stepped back a foot, a gun in hand. "You first," the gaunt-faced man said. Fargo rose, stepped from the wagon, thought about making a dive for safety, but knew those behind him or the driver would pour bullets into him. He stepped down and saw the swift-rushing, small river only a few paces away.

The other three men came up behind him, and Fargo realized what they were about to do. But he didn't steel muscles and tense his body to receive the blow. Instead, he did the opposite, let his body relax to the edge of going limp. Muscles responded and nerves followed, quieted, all normal resistance diminishing. It was a technique taught him by a Crow medicine man he had befriended, and it had saved his life before, even when it didn't completely work. It involved every aspect of the body abandoning its normal reaction and resistance to pain. Instead, the body absorbed pain, and by absorbing it, lessened its impact. "The tree that bends does not receive the full force of the wind. The tree that does not bend breaks," the shaman had told him. Fargo grimaced as he heard the soft swish of air, an arm descending fast and hard.

The blow was a sharp explosion of pain that shot through his head. He felt himself topple forward, the world fading away, yet he kept himself relaxed. Cold wetness struck at him, engulfed him. But he was aware until, in moments, the curtain of grayness swept over him, wrapping him in an opaque blanket. Vision vanished, sound disappeared, sensation slipped away. Yet final, complete unconsciousness did not sweep him into an embrace that usually led to death. Somehow, he was aware of being carried downriver, swept along by the swift current. Water was beginning to fill his lungs when he surfaced and automatically gasped in breaths of air. The darkness was more than the night as he was swept along on the surface of the river.

Once again the body reacted automatically, the instinct of survival taking over. But it was made possible only because unconsciousness had not completely taken over. Though the darkness still held him, he felt his arms move, feeble attempts to swim, yet not without some success. Wetness splashed his face, cold invigoration, and he managed to open his eyes. He saw nothing at first, and then in little glimpses forms and shapes began to arrange themselves. A bank of high brush appeared, then a line of trees. His arms took on strength and began to propel him forward with purpose. A low hanging black willow branch loomed up before him. He reached up, caught hold of it, and clung to it as it swayed with his weight. Peering into the dark, he saw the shoreline less than a dozen feet away, then let himself slide from the branch. He hit the water, paddled, and felt the soft shore beneath his feet. He staggered from the water, lay on the shore, and gasped in air.

Finally, he crawled to the line of brush back from the edge of the shore. He'd been swept downriver at once. His assailants were satisfied they'd killed him, but he didn't want to take any chances. He stayed in the brush for another half hour, and when no figures appeared searching along the opposite shore, he rose, shivering in the wet clothes. A glance skyward showed a moon on its way to the horizon. He pulled off his soaked clothes, spread each piece atop brush and branches, and moved naked into the line of sycamore. Without the wet clothes the warm night let him dry without shivering, and he leaned back against a tree trunk, drew in deep breaths, and silently gave thanks to an old Crow medicine man.

He fell asleep, woke when the sun rose, and stayed where he was, estimating the sun would take an hour to dry his clothes and returned to sleep. He woke again after the hour had gone by, and his clothes were dry. He dressed and stepped out into the open, then walked to the shore. His eyes slowly swept the countryside. A furrow slid across his brow. He surveyed the land again and took in the narrow path that ran east from the river some hundred yards up, the house that faced the shoreline a dozen yards beyond. His glance went back to an oak-lined road and the large house at the end of it. He had seen the road and the house before. Only once, but it was enough. His was the Trailsman's mind. Things once seen imprinted themselves on it, as notes imprint themselves on a musician's mind.

"Chantilly Road," he murmured aloud and began to walk toward the house at the far end. The front door opened as he approached, and Linda emerged, staring at him.

"This is a surprise," she said.

"For both of us," he answered.

"You going to leave it at that?" she asked.

"Some unfriendly gents threw me into the river last night," he said. "I need a ride back to the hotel."

"That's easy enough," Linda said. "Why'd they go after you?"

"Didn't want me to keep a date," Fargo said, his eyes sweeping the scene. "I'm wondering why they brought me here to do me in."

"This is a pretty isolated area. The river's often used to get rid of people," Linda said. "They're always fishing out bodies." She paused. "You thinking maybe they figured to send me a message, too?"

"It was a thought," Fargo said. "Somebody knew what I was supposed to do. They could've seen us together."

"I'll get my horse," Linda said, walked behind the house, and came back with the gray mare. Fargo swung onto the horse behind her. "Hotel Plymouth," he said.

Linda gave a smug smile. "Now that I know where, maybe you ought to tell me who and why," she said.

"I'm thinking the less you know the safer you'll be," Fargo said.

"I don't care about being safe. I care about justice," she said, her unswerving determination instantly surfacing. He didn't pursue the subject as she moved onto the Washington streets and finally reached the hotel, where he slid from the mare.

"Thanks," he said.

"What about your meeting?" Linda asked.

"I expect to keep it," Fargo said, then paused. "Maybe I can tell you more afterward," he said. "Maybe."

She sniffed, allowing him a tolerant half smile, then rode away. He went into the hotel, where the elderly clerk rose at once. "That man was here looking for you last night," the clerk said. "He waited over an hour, finally left."

"Thanks," Fargo said, and hurried to the stable. Minutes later, he was astride the Ovaro, riding hard as he returned to the river. He halted at the south bank, his eyes scanning the shoreline. It wasn't hard to find the wheel marks, the distinctive cut made by the gouges in the left rear wheel of the carriage. After throwing him into the river and leaving him for dead, they had turned and rode back along the bank, turning onto the small path before joining the hard-packed road. He followed the wheel marks with ease, seeing the way the carriage had rolled back toward Washington.

It had reached the outskirts of the capital, where the streets were not yet cobbled, and he saw the tracks curve sharply west. He followed the tracks along dirt streets that led into a shabby section of the capital, the houses wood and tar paper, some of poorly laid brick. He took note of unkempt front yards and slovenly-looking children as he followed the wheel marks. Then houses stood farther apart, and stands of box elder rose up to obscure some of them. When the tracks curved alongside a thick stand of trees, Fargo drew to a halt and swung from his horse. The day had drifted into afternoon, and the sun was on its path to the horizon. He tied the Ovaro to a tree, well back in the wooded stand, then pulled the big Henry from its saddle case and continued on foot. He stayed at the edge of the trees, where he could see the wheel treads that moved alongside the woods, and had moved another few thousand yards when he froze, his eyes peering at a ramshackle house.

The black carriage rested in front, unhitched, its broken lamp a mocking reminder. Fargo's eyes scanned the house and saw tattered curtains drawn over the windows. But he saw no signs of anyone, heard no sounds. Staying in the trees, he moved past the house and saw the horse tethered behind the structure. Returning to the front of the house, he dropped to one knee and settled down to wait as the day drew to an end. They were inside, he was certain, and his certainty was satisfied as night came and a lamp went on inside. They were there, and he could think of only one reason why. They were waiting for someone. Once again, his assumption proved right as, perhaps another hour later, a man rode up, halted, and swung form his horse.

Fargo peered at the man, but darkness cloaked most of the figure. The door of the house opened, and Fargo saw the gaunt-faced man come out. The visitor followed him into the house, and the door had barely closed when Fargo was on one knee beside the nearest window. He peered through the long tears in the tattered curtains and saw the four men and the newcomer. As he watched, the gaunt-faced one drew the Colt from his pocket, held it up, and turned it in his hand for the visitor. *Goddamn*, Fargo swore silently. The man was presenting proof that they had done their job. The visitor took an envelope from his pocket, handed it to the gaunt-faced man, and turned for the door. Fargo bolted in a crouch back in the trees as the visitor emerged and rode away. Fargo let the sound of the horse fade before he took another grip on the rifle and started toward the house.

He moved in a crouch, stopping just below the windowsill, and raised the butt of his rifle. A quick glance through the window showed the four men dividing the money. Swinging the rifle butt in a short arc, he smashed it through the window and was rewarded with a shower of glass and shouts of surprise. Staying below the windowsill, he called out, "You shouldn't take money for a job you didn't do." He heard the collective hiss of shock and surprise.

"Sonofabitch," the curse followed. Fargo hunkered down farther, certain of what would follow. He stayed against the wall as the barrage of shots hurtled through the window, accompanied by barrage of curses. Keeping low, Fargo backed away from the window, halted at the corner of the house, and raised the rifle. Silence settled over the house, and Fargo waited, the rifle ready to fire. He caught the sound of murmured exchanges. They were trying to decide whether they'd gotten him with the barrage. Finally, he caught movement at the doorway and saw the door slowly open. One of the men edged out and peered across the darkness.

Fargo pressed the trigger, and the big Henry barked. The figure in the doorway flew backward, his feet leaving the ground. He hit the door, crumpled, and rolled into a lifeless ball. The door swung shut. Another wave of bullets hurtled through the smashed window, an exercise in frustration more than fear. When they stopped shooting, Fargo raised his voice again. "Throw your guns out. Save us both a lot of time," he called. Another shot answered him. "I want to talk," Fargo said. "Talk and you live. No talk and you're dead."

"Come in and get us," a voice snarled.

"I just told you the deal. Take it. Don't be dumber than you are," Fargo said.

"Come get us," the voice snarled again.

"I'll wait," Fargo said.

"So will we," another voice said. "Come morning, you're dead, mister, this time for good."

Fargo didn't reply, but he swore silently. Come morning they'd have a real advantage. The house had a second floor. They could each take a window and look down at him. He'd be the target if he stayed anywhere in the open. He'd have to retreat to the trees if he wanted to stay alive, and the trees afforded a poor line of fire. Thoughts raced as he heard the men inside moving about, settling down to wait. He stayed back, his eyes moving up and down the ramshackle structure. There was no place for him to climb to the second floor, only a hanging, broken drainpipe that wouldn't possibly support him. He surveyed the first floor and saw nothing that would let him sneak into the house.

His eyes traveled across the base of the building and saw splintered boards, jagged-edged moldings, cracked pieces of siding. Dry brush and weeds had grown along the base of the house, as if nature tried to mask the disrepair of the place. But suddenly Fargo's eyes narrowed. He couldn't let the three killers stay in the house and wait for morning, and they surely weren't about to come out on their own. They obviously felt confident that all they had to do was wait. "Guess again," Fargo murmured as he lay the rifle on the ground and, staying low to the ground, moved to the corner of the house. Reaching into his pocket, he drew out a long lucifer, lighted the match, and crouched at the base of the dry and rotted sideboards. He let the fire seize the dry brush also, taking a little longer but finally catching onto the edges of the splintered boards. Once it took hold, the flames leaped eagerly, running up the dry old wood almost with glee. Keeping very low to the ground, he half crawled, half slid along the front of the house, pausing to light more fire where the boards were particularly splintered and welcoming.

It took only minutes before the flames were crawling up the sides of the house, fueling themselves first on the dry brush, then on the dry wood. He crawled back to where he'd left the rifle, picked up the gun, and watched, astonished at how quickly the flames devoured the wood and became a leaping, raging channel of fire. Smoke began to curl upward through the smashed window and the cracks in the house. It took a few more moments, but finally Fargo heard the shouts, consternation at first, then panic. The fire had reached the top of the front of the house and had begun to consume the sides. Fargo heard the sound of glass breaking on the second floor.

He waited on one knee, the big Henry raised to shoot, and heard the shouts from inside the house, curses and accusations and more curses. Suddenly, a figure appeared at the window alongside the door, a bucket in hand. The man leaned out and tossed water on the line of flame alongside the window. The flames hissed and went out at the spot, and the man swung his legs over the windowsill. Fargo let the big Henry explode, and the man shuddered as he hung half out the window. The bucket fell from his hands, and his upper body toppled backward into the house while his legs hung lifelessly over the windowsill. The door flew open, its front wreathed in flames. A figure raced from the house, diving when it cleared the doorway. The rifle barked again, and the figure hit the ground and lay still.

Fargo waited, his eyes sweeping the house from side to side. Smoke and flame were enveloping the structure now, and he heard glass smashing from a side window. He rose, ran, and reached the side of the house just in time to see the gaunt-faced man leaping from a second-floor window. Two bullets hit him before he hit the ground. Fargo trotted past the flaming house and made his way to the trees. He turned back suddenly to where the man had leaped from the side window, ducking from flames as he reached the figure, knelt down, and retrieved the Colt from the man's waist. This time he kept going until he reached the Ovaro.

It hadn't turned out the way he'd wanted. He had no answers. But he was very alive, and the night was still young. He hadn't met John Nicolay, but Ben Stott had told him to appear at a fancy formal ball. It was often considered fashionable to make a late entrance, he reminded himself as he climbed onto the Ovaro and rode back to the heart of Washington.

6

Fargo rode to the hotel, changed to a fresh outfit, and asked directions of the desk clerk. "The Jeffers house? Everybody in Washington society knows the Jeffers house. Right on Park Road," the clerk said. Fargo nodded thanks and rode the pinto through the Washington night, lamplights reflecting in the Potomac. When he drew up to Park Road, he found a brilliantly lighted mansion, where music drifted out from the open terraced windows. Up an expansive driveway in an adjoining lot he saw an array of panel boot victorias, full clarences, broughams, peabody victorias, and landaulettes, along with round bottom bretts, stanhope phaetons, and chariots. High society had indeed turned out for the affair, he took note. He halted and swung from the saddle as a boy clothed in mock Turkish costume took the Ovaro's cheekstrap. "We'll see to your horse, sir," he said, and Fargo handed him the reins.

As the boy walked the pinto away, Fargo strode to the open front door of the mansion, where an elderly black man in a formal cutaway frock coat greeted him with polite firmness. "Your invitation, please," he said.

"Please tell Miss Jeffers or Mister Nicolay that the Trailsman is here," Fargo said. The man called someone from the floor and conveyed the message. Fargo waited to one side and watched the huge room filled with men and women in evening clothes, most dancing to a string orchestra in the background. He was also aware of some curious stares from some of the well-dressed crowd. It took a few minutes, but finally a figure came toward him, surrounded by swirls of gold lamé. She glided as if propelled on air, a vision wrapped in shimmering gold that halted and stared at him, a furrow creasing her lovely, smooth brow.

Fargo stared back at one of the most beautiful women he had ever seen. Long flame red hair hung below her shoulders, a fiery frame for a gorgeous face, each feature as perfect as the next, eyes green as agate, nose straight and thin, flaring ever so slightly at the tip, finely etched lips that were both patrician yet sensuous. The gold lamé gown exposed bare lovely shoulders and bare arms, and a very, very low décolletage revealed almost all of her beautifully curved, smooth breasts. "I'm Cornelia Jeffers," she said in a low, purring voice that matched the rest of her. "Please come with me."

She spun in a graceful motion and floated away. He hurried after her into a room off to the side and found himself in a wood-paneled study with what appeared to be family portraits on the walls and deep cushioned furniture gracing the floor behind a fine antique desk. Cornelia Jeffers closed the door, and he watched the way her breasts dipped as she moved, yet the gown stayed absolutely in place. She turned to face him, her eyes wide. "Good God, we thought you'd been killed," she said.

"We?" Fargo queried.

"John Nicolay and myself. The desk clerk told him three men took you outside with them," Cornelia Jeffers said in her low, purring voice.

"They tried," Fargo said laconically as Cornelia studied him with an appraising glance.

"You're apparently everything they say about you."

He was going to ask questions when there was a knock and the door opened. A man entered, dark brown hair, a young face, probably not much more than thirty, Fargo guessed, tall, handsome in a quiet way, nothing outstanding about his features. He closed the door after him, his attention on Fargo. "John Nicolay," he said. "I didn't believe my ears when Cornelia had me called from the French ambassador's table."

"I'm here, but I'm not happy," Fargo grunted. "I've been lied to, dry-gulched, pistol-whipped, tossed in a river, and shot at, and that's only part of it. I want to know why, or I'm riding west."

"I don't blame you for being annoyed," John Nicolay said.

"Try mad as hell," Fargo interrupted.

Nicolay nodded and had the sensitivity to look uncomfortable. "Yes, of course," he murmured. "The meeting we never had will take place tomorrow morning. I'll come for you."

"Not good enough. I want something to hang my hat on now, such as who are you?" Fargo demanded.

"I am secretary to Mr. Abraham Lincoln," John Nicolay said. Fargo felt his eyebrows lift. "President Lincoln will be at our meeting. Will that be enough for now?" Nicolay said.

Fargo's lips pursed as he wrestled with the surprise that had come over him. "Guess that'll hold me," he conceded, then turned to Cornelia Jeffers. "Where do you fit in with this?" he asked.

John Nicolay answered. "That will be explained tomorrow, along with everything else. Meanwhile, let's say that Cornelia is very important to us."

Cornelia Jeffers stepped to Fargo and slipped her arm inside his. "We must get back to my guests. Come along and have something to eat," she said.

"I could use that," Fargo said, the mention of food triggering his hunger. With Cornelia Jeffers still holding his arm, he followed John Nicolay from the room and into the huge festive ballroom, where he took in the great chandeliers and draperies that swept the room. Nicolay went on to where a half dozen men and women were at a table, and Cornelia steered the way through dancing couples to a long buffet table piled high with everything from chicken to Maryland crabs.

"You look like a beef sandwich man to me, Fargo," she said, relinquishing her hold of his arm.

"That'd be fine," he said, and Cornelia nodded to

two men behind the table who immediately began to make the sandwich.

"Bourbon," she said to one of the men.

Fargo smiled at her. "How'd you know?" he asked.

"One doesn't become the leading hostess in Washington without being able to match a man to his drink," she said, and laughed, a low, lovely sound. His eyes couldn't help traveling across the creamy white smoothness of her breasts as they dipped when she turned. The flame red hair brought his gaze to her perfect face and agate green eyes.

"I don't know about the leading hostess, but I'll bet you're the most beautiful," he said.

Her smile dazzled. "I'll take that as a special compliment from someone who sees in ways most men don't," she said as the waiter served him his sandwich. He had taken a bite and sipped from the bourbon also handed him when he saw a figure coming toward Cornelia. The man approached on quick steps, clothed in an expensively tailored cutaway coat. Fargo took in a slightly portly build, the coat unable to conceal a paunch. The man had a soft face, a prominent nose, a mouth that turned down at the corners, and thinning dark brown hair. He was followed by a slightly taller man with blondish hair, clothed in a black dress coat, a purple sash, and a row of medals pinned on one lapel. Cornelia extended her hand to the first man and flicked a quick glance at Fargo. "Prince Napoleon, special envoy from the government of France, and his aide-de-camp, Monsieur Camille Ferri Pisano," she said. The name prodded

Fargo into seeing the resemblance to Emperor Bonaparte as the prince obviously tried to further the comparison by carrying one hand tucked into his vest.

"Miss Jeffers, how good to see you again," the prince said to Cornelia with a charm plainly more practiced than real.

"I'm honored you could come." Cornelia smiled radiantly. "This is Mister Skye Fargo. He's visiting from the Western territories," she said.

"How nice," the portly little man said in barely polite dismissal, all his attention on Cornelia. "You know I wouldn't miss one of your parties if I could help it. Of course, I'm eager to know what you think about the American attitude toward France. Mr. Nicolay is so full of political platitudes. I learn so little from him, but you always know the latest inside gossip, and you're never afraid to speak your mind."

"I'm told the American government wants to keep France as a friend," Cornelia said.

"What do you hear about this man Lincoln?" the prince asked.

"We're meeting with him tomorrow," the aide-decamp put in.

"I hear so many conflicting things about him," the prince said, his probing quite transparent.

"He's a complicated man," Cornelia said. "Complicated men impress different people differently."

Fargo smiled. Cornelia was an expert at parrying oblique questions, he noted.

"I hear he does not understand compromise, not as we do in France," the prince said.

"Nobody understands compromise as the French do," Cornelia said, her smile almost taking the burn out of her reply, though Fargo saw Ferri Pisano's face stiffen.

The prince took her arm. "Let us sit down. I want to hear more about this man Lincoln," he said, and started to steer her toward a sofa against the wall. Fargo caught the quick glance Cornelia threw him.

"Please enjoy the party, Fargo. We'll be meeting again," she said. He nodded back as she swirled away with Prince Napoleon, Ferri Pisano following along and looking like a well-dressed puppy. Fargo strolled through the revelers, enjoying the music as he sipped another bourbon. He tried to find John Nicolay, but didn't see him anywhere in the crowd. The man's mention of Abraham Lincoln had taken him completely by surprise, Fargo realized. But then surprises seemed very much a part of this venture. A flash of blue organdy with red bows brushed against him.

"Hello," the voice said, and Fargo turned, astonishment sweeping through him as he stared at the short, dark blond hair and dark blue eyes. "Surprised?" she asked.

"That's putting it mildly," he said.

"I told you the family used to travel in high society," Linda said. "I still go to an occasional party."

He leveled a skeptical glance at her. "You're not here to play party girl."

She shrugged. "Cornelia's parties are famous. You can hear everything important to hear and see everything important to see," she said.

"Have you done that?" he questioned.

"Found you here. That means something," she replied.

"I don't know what it means, not yet," he said, and let his eyes scan her dress. "You're looking very attractive."

She gave him a slightly chiding smile. "After you've met Cornelia, no one's attractive. Every woman in Washington has learned that," Linda said a little sorrowfully. "Too bad, really. Beauty is a wonderful mask."

"You're not fond of Cornelia?" Fargo asked.

"I've known her too long," Linda said, and Fargo smiled inwardly.

"That sounds suspiciously like jealousy," he commented.

"Only part of it," she sniffed.

"What's the rest?"

"She and her family have always been too thick with the government for my tastes," Linda said.

"Oh, yes, you don't trust the government. It doesn't keep its word, you said," Fargo recalled.

"That's right," she snapped. "It seems you don't, either. You promised to tell me things."

"I didn't promise. I said maybe, if I learned anything to help you. I haven't yet," he said.

"No matter. Nothing's changed. I'm looking on my own till I get answers," Linda said. "Come see me when you're ready to talk."

She spun on her heel and plunged into the crowd, and he watched her accept an invitation to dance. He turned away, moved through the crowd, and went outside. The attendant brought the Ovaro, and Fargo rode back through the late night. At the hotel he stabled the horse, went to his room, and stretched out in the darkness. A woman of flame red hair and consummate beauty swam into his thoughts until he dropped off to sleep.

Morning brought the sun to wake him, and he had just finished a cup of coffee and a biscuit in the hotel lobby when John Nicolay appeared. "Glad you're up and ready," Nicolay said and led the way to a dark red brougham, where a driver and a uniformed guard waited. Nicolay was silent during the short trip that ended when they drew up before a modest house with two white columns. Not far from it Fargo glimpsed the impressive Capitol building with the dome still unfinished. Nicolay led the way inside the house to a spacious, book-lined study with thick half-drawn curtains of deep maroon. The figure at the desk rose as they entered and seemed to take minutes to stop rising.

"President Lincoln," John Nicolay said by way of introduction, and Fargo took in the tall figure that seemed to have been carved out of a tamarack, long and spare, somehow exuding the very spirit of backwoods America. A long, lean face bore an almost sad kindliness, as if its craggy features bore the weight of the nation's troubles. And they did, Fargo reminded himself. A simple black suit added to Abraham Lincoln's quietly imposing presence, and the new president of the country walked toward him with a piece of paper in one hand.

"Glad you've come, Fargo. I've been told all about you," Lincoln said. "These are difficult times, sad times. If you can help us, you'll be doing your country a favor it can never repay."

"I'll try my best," Fargo said.

"Captain John Winslow is going to join us soon. He and John will brief you on the practical aspects of our problem. But I believe a man does his best work when he knows why he's asked to serve, and what the people around him stand for. I want to give you the background of what's hanging over the United States," Lincoln said, and moved closer to Fargo, leaning his long frame against the sturdy wooden desk. "There are forces that would destroy the United States as we know it, as it was founded. They want to secede from the Union. They have taken their issues and used them as their rallying cry. If they succeed, the Union will be destroyed. I cannot let this happen. Keeping the Union together is my first priority."

"I've heard talk, rumors, but I didn't know things had gone this far," Fargo said.

"This far and farther," the president said, and held up the piece of paper in his hand. "This is a passage from a speech. I want to have your reaction to it." He began to read, his voice clear and measured: "We are not enemies, but friends. We must not be enemies. Though passion may have strained, it must not break, our bonds of affection. The mystic chords of memory, stretching from every battlefield and patriot grave to every living heart . . . will yet swell the chorus of the Union when again touched, as surely they will be, by the better angels of our nature."

He halted and lowered the paper in his hand, his eyes held on Fargo. "What did you get from that, Fargo? Be honest. I appreciate honesty," Lincoln said.

"A man trying to appeal to both sides," Fargo said.

Abraham Lincoln's face found a smile. "Exactly. But unfortunately it didn't work," he said.

"It seldom does. It's hard to sit on a fence. You usually have to get down and take a position," Fargo said.

"The wisdom of the prairies," Lincoln remarked. "I have taken a position. Keep the Union intact. Prevent secession. That is my first priority. I have often expressed my personal wish that all men be free. The idea of one man owning another is repugnant to me. But if I could save the Union without freeing any slave, I would do it; and if I could save the Union by freeing all the slaves, I would do it; and if I could save it by freeing some slaves and leaving others, I would also do that. Preserving the Union must come first. All other rightful things will in time follow." He paused, reached back, and took a sip of water from a glass behind him. "Whether I can preserve the Union looks more and more uncertain. I hope you can help me succeed, Fargo."

John Nicolay turned at a knock at the door and admitted a man in a naval captain's uniform. Fargo took in graying hair atop a square face, tanned and sharp-eyed. The captain snapped a sharp salute to the president. "Good morning, Captain," Lincoln said.

"Skye Fargo, this is Captain John Winslow of the United States Navy," Nicolay introduced. "The captain is aware why you were brought in. I think it best if he starts our briefing."

"There's a war going on, Fargo," the captain said, and smiled at the surprise that crossed Fargo's face. "No one's called it that yet. A lot of people aren't even aware of it. But it's going on, and it's a war. The secessionist forces need money. They are unfortunately getting it through the cooperation of the British. Every British merchantman that picks up a hold full of cotton, tobacco, peanuts, and lumber adds hundreds of thousands of dollars to the secessionist treasury. As the British need the cotton and other things, it becomes a mutual benefit to both."

"We established a blockade to prevent British merchantmen from reaching secessionist ports. It has had some success, but not nearly enough. The other side has its own frigates that fight our ships and help the English blockade runners," John Nicolay put in. "Yet we have been holding our own. We consider we're doing well when we can stop half the British merchantmen from getting through. But suddenly we have been in real trouble."

"Somehow, the secessionist forces have been attacking our warships with a collection of very small, very fast, and very effective vessels," Captain Winslow took up. "Sloop-rigged cutters, they swarm in, fire, and escape before our warships can hit back. They carry a ten-inch cannon at the bow and another at the stern. They're like mosquitoes. I've never seen vessels so small and so effective. They've sunk two dozen of our ships. That translates into fifty more British merchantmen getting through the blockade. They're too small to make an Atlantic crossing on their own, and they wouldn't bring them in by ship."

"Why not?" Fargo queried.

"They wouldn't dare. If we uncovered the ships on a merchantman during one of our searches, it'd prove the involvement of the British government. They can't risk that. No, these little ships are being brought in overland. That's why we've called on you, Fargo."

"It'd seem easy enough to find a ship being moved, even a little one, but apparently not," the captain said. "We've had others try, and they've all failed. Some have been murdered. There are a lot of secessionist agents and sympathizers out there."

"No leads?" Fargo questioned.

"One. A disgruntled sailor from a schooner said he heard about ships being brought in up north around Philadelphia. But to bring them all the way down here seems impossible. We've people watching every inch of the shore."

"They're not bringing them by shore. They know your people will be watching for that. I'd guess they go west to the Tuscarora Mountains and down into the Shenandoah Valley," Fargo said.

"Without being seen? How?" the captain asked.

"Maybe moving only by night. I don't know," Fargo said.

"I want you to see these little cutters for yourself, so you'll know what you're looking for. I want you to come aboard with me, be there when they attack. They will. They're being very aggressive," Captain Winslow said.

"Let's go," Fargo said, then turned as Abraham Lincoln stepped toward him.

"Good luck, Fargo. I've every confidence in you," the tall, craggy figure said.

"Thanks." Fargo nodded and left with the captain and John Nicolay. Outside, he saw a dark blue post chaise with a naval insignia on the door.

"We'll stop at the hotel and get your things. We'll see that your horse is taken care of while you're at sea," the captain said.

"I'll be going off on my own afterward," Fargo said. "How do I report in if I come across something?"

"Directly if you must, but Cornelia Jeffers can be your contact," Nicolay said.

"Where does she fit in?" Fargo asked.

"Cornelia Jeffers is our top agent. With her family background in both the North and the South, she's in the perfect position to help us. You can trust Cornelia as you would the president and myself, but she's the only one," Nicolay said.

Fargo nodded, stepped into the carriage with the captain, and sat back. At the hotel he took his saddlebag and the big Henry. "Handsome rifle," Captain Winslow said. "Though we don't do much rifle shooting at sea."

"Maybe you should," Fargo said, and smiled. The

carriage rolled on to the shore of the Potomac, then followed the river south past Alexandria, down along the long curve to where it finally stopped at Colonial Beach. A longboat waited there with six crewmen who rowed them to a large ship moored midriver. Fargo took in its combination of beauty and power, his eyes lingering on the gun ports painted white against the black hull.

"The frigate *Independence*," Captain Winslow said as they came alongside the vessel. "Three-masted, full-rigged, and skysails and main moonsail. A good, sturdy vessel." Fargo climbed up the rope ladder, then swung himself over the rail onto the deck. A young officer greeted him with a crisp salute.

"Lieutenant Carr. Welcome aboard," he said.

"Prepare to sail, Mr. Carr," the captain said, and the younger officer hurried away. The captain led Fargo along the deck, gesturing to the row of cannon on the port and starboard sides of the ship. "Twenty-four twelve-inch guns and six eight-inch," the captain said. "We can mount a tremendous broadside." He led Fargo down a short companionway into a small cabin. "A little cramped, but that's life at sea. Besides, you won't be with us too long. I'll be topside if you need anything," the captain said, and climbed up to the deck. Fargo felt the ship moving, heard the sound of the waves against the hull, and sat down on the hard bunk for a moment. He knew why he'd been called here, at last understanding what they expected of him.

It seemed ridiculously easy on the face of it. A ship, even a small one, should be no problem to find.

/et he knew better. Others had tried, paid for trying with their lives, and failed. He never discounted history. The search would be far from easy. A clever scheme was being cleverly executed. For now he'd stand with his evaluation. The little ships were being smuggled in under cover of the Appalachians, then at the shortest route moved to the Virginia waterways, perhaps the Rappahannock or the upper reaches of the James or the Pamunkey. Feeling the ship pick up speed, he turned off speculation and climbed up onto the deck.

Busy sailors scrambled up and down rigging, adjusting sails under barked commands. Fargo saw the ship had reached Chesapeake Bay and begun to sail downward toward the entrance to the Atlantic. He walked to where Captain Winslow stood with a telescope in hand. A smaller vessel raised its sails as they neared and began to move forward a hundred yards ahead. "Our escort vessel, the schooner *Freedom*," the captain said. "She doesn't carry our armament, but she's faster." Fargo felt the sea wind on his face as the ship reached the ocean, slowly curving its way seaward. The sun dropped toward the horizon, he noted, and the frigate moved with only half its sails raised. The schooner, sleeker of lines, but with its gun ports also painted white, stayed its hundred yards ahead. Fargo felt the long, rolling swells of the ocean lift the ship, cradle it, and send it on with another gentle lift. They were in the Atlantic, beyond sight of shore, and the sun was just touching the horizon line when

Fargo heard Captain Winslow's shout, the telescope to his eye.

"All hands to gun ports," the captain ordered. Fargo peered across the water, straining his eyes, and suddenly saw the tall, white shapes rising up from the water, first one, then another, till he'd counted six. The frigate resounded to the pounding of feet and cannons being readied, gunnery seamen positioning cannon shot, casings, powder, and ramrods. The captain shouted more commands, and a dozen figures climbed up the rigging of the mainmast. Moments later, Fargo saw the square sail unfurl. His eyes went back to the sea. The white shapes had become ships, small, sleek little ships each with a single mast. He knew enough to recognize sloops, a single mast with a jib and a mainsail.

They were coming on fast, spreading apart he saw, and Captain Winslow's voice called out. "Come about. Prepare to fire starboard broadside," he ordered. The frigate began to turn, and Fargo's face creased at the slowness of the maneuver. Four of the small, attacking sloops were aiming at the schooner, and Fargo watched them aim at it from both sides, then do a fast come about and skitter away as the schooner's guns fired and missed. Instantly, two of the sloops turned while the other two raced to come up at the schooner's stern. Fargo watched as the two nearest attackers came in from the bow and fired. He saw their shots hit the schooner on the foredeck. The foremast toppled, slowly at first, then crashed onto the deck. He could see the ship shudder, and then the two attackers near the stern fired, and another two shots smashed into the larger vessel. This time the stern of the schooner broke away, a gaping hole into which the sea immediately poured.

Fargo's eyes went to the attackers. They had turned and were heeling away, each in a separate direction. They had hit and run, hit again and run. Not unlike a Cheyenne attack on a heavily armored wagon train, he noted. Suddenly, there was a tremendous explosion as the frigate fired broadside. The ship reverberated, and Fargo grabbed hold of the rail to stay upright. But he saw one of the two sloops sailing in a half circle, untouched. He turned and saw the other coming directly at the frigate from the bow. The little ship fired, and the shot hurtled into the frigate just below the bow rail. The ship shuddered, and Fargo found himself on one knee, still clinging to the rail with one hand. He pulled himself up and saw the sloop had made a smart, tight turn and was sailing away from another broadside.

He saw four figures aboard the attacker, one at the bow gun, one at the stern gun, one at the tiller, and the fourth handling the mainsail. Running in a crouch, skipping over torn pieces of rope on the deck, he made it to the cabin, grabbed the rifle, and climbed up on deck again. He ran to the rail at the stern; this time saw both of the little attackers coming in directly astern. He saw the frigate turning to bring its guns to bear in another broadside, sailors valiantly pulling at ropes to get the most out of each sail. But they'd never bring the ship around in time, he saw. He steadied the big Henry atop the rail, drew a bead on the man at the tiller of the nearest sloop, and fired. The figure catapulted backward over the side of the ship, and Fargo saw the man at the mainsail take a hitch with the mainsheet around a belaying pin and dive for the tiller. He never reached it as Fargo's shot caught him midway. The sloop had almost spun in a turn, aimless with only the wind controlling it.

It headed directly for its companion attacker. Fargo saw the tiller man on the second sloop rise and yank hard to turn away. The rifle exploded again, and the man fell backward, arms outspread. The sloop almost halted, the sails shaking, as the other sloop rammed it from the side. Both vessels came apart even as they were jammed together. Fargo fired again, and another of the men fell, hit the splintered side of the sloop, and slid into the sea. A roar of cannon exploded, and Fargo saw the two sloops blown skyward as the broadside hurled into them.

He peered across at the schooner. The ship was down at the stern, taking water fast. The four attackers turned smartly, broke into two groups of two each, and bore down on the frigate. Once again Captain Winslow wheeled his vessel to bring its big guns to bear. But they'd be too slow Fargo saw as the attackers began to come in from the bow and the stern. Steadying himself against the stern rail, he watched the two sloops come boring in, waited as long as he dared, then fired, choosing the tiller man on the right-hand ship. The man fell across his tiller, pushing it to one side. The sloop's bow turned, a crazy, shuddering maneuver, directly across the path of the other sloop. The seaman on the second sloop yanked at his tiller to try to turn away. The big Henry's crack ended his attempt. His ship ran into the other squarely amidships, both breaking apart like so many pieces of packing crate.

They were almost underwater when the frigate's big guns blasted away what was left of them. Fargo's eyes went along the deck, past the bow, and saw the two remaining sloops racing away as fast as the wind would permit. He sought out the schooner and saw its stern completely underwater. Lifeboats had been lowered, some already moving toward the frigate. Fargo put the rifle down as Captain Winslow came toward him. "By God, rifles instead of cannon. I've learned something today, thanks to you, Fargo. If we can slow them down with rifle fire, we'll have time to bring our big guns around," he said excitedly.

"It'll help you," Fargo said.

"I'm ordering a rifle squad on every ship we send out," Winslow said. "Of course, they won't all be your kind of marksman, but we'll do our best."

"They'll figure a way to fight back, of course," Fargo said.

"That's always the way. Meanwhile, we'll do better than we have."

"How much damage do you have?" Fargo asked.

"Superstructure—nothing that can't be repaired," the captain said, and Fargo saw the crew of the schooner being taken aboard as the last of the day slid away. "We'll head to port and get you back to your place," Winslow said. "Any new thoughts now that you've seen the ships?"

"Nothing that makes it easier to understand. But I still say the Appalachians are the only way they could be sneaked in. That's where I'll be tracking," Fargo said.

"Thanks again for today, Fargo. I'll see that John Nicolay hears about this," Captain Winslow said. "You've survived your first battle on the high seas. Congratulations."

"I'll take the high plains. I only have to worry about arrows, not drowning, too," Fargo said. The captain's laugh followed him as he leaned over the rail and let the night sea wind blow over him as the ship sailed back up the Chesapeake, turned into the mouth of the Potomac, and hove to as a longboat deposited him at Colonial Beach.

A naval carriage waited there, then drove him back to the Washington hotel by a little past midnight. He undressed in his room and stretched out on the bed. He went to sleep certain of only one thing: The trail he'd been sent to find might or might not be the hardest he'd ever have to unravel, but it would certainly be the strangest.

7

When Fargo went downstairs with the new morning, the desk clerk handed him a note. "Messenger delivered it real early," the clerk said. Fargo opened it and stared down at the single line on the paper.

Important you stop here first. Cornelia J.

He pocketed the note and went to the stable, finding the Ovaro brushed and fed. "Miss me?" he asked as he saddled up and received a vigorous nod that shook the silky mane. He rode the Washington streets past fancy carriages and delivery wagons and saw the front door open as he pulled up before the Jeffers mansion. Cornelia stepped out, no swirling, décolléte evening dress now, but a cream-colored tailored shirt and black jodhpurs. But her striking beauty wasn't diminished. It merely took on a new dimension. The flame red hair fell gently against the cream-colored shirt, drawn tight by full, deep breasts. Her agate green eyes sparkled, and the black jodhpurs were so form fitting they could have been sewn on.

" 'Morning, Fargo," Cornelia Jeffers said, flashing her dazzling smile. His eyes went to the handsome buckskin a stable boy brought around from behind the mansion. "We're going riding," Cornelia said as she climbed onto the horse with a graceful motion that let him see a very round, full rear. The deep breasts dipped in unison as she swung into the saddle. He brought the Ovaro beside her, and she started off in a trot. "Now you know why you're here," she said. "You're going searching in the Appalachians, I'm told. John Nicolay briefed me," she said before he could ask.

"I figure to start looking west of the end of the James," Fargo said.

"That'd be at the Virginia ridge. Good. I'm taking you to a large cabin at the very edge of the mountains. It's a safe house. We've used it for meetings. You can use it when you're tired tramping about the mountains, and it's a place we can reach you," Cornelia said.

"We?" Fargo inquired. "I've already learned not to trust strangers."

"That's right. We will mostly mean me. Only a few people know it exists. John Nicolay is one. The president is another," Cornelia said.

"So you think," Fargo grunted.

She tossed him a smile. "I'm more than confident, but I'm glad you're a skeptic," she said, and he fell behind her as she took a very narrow passage, then came back alongside her when it widened. "How'd you get into this?" Fargo asked.

"They asked me," she answered. "I've always had a taste for adventure, for doing something dangerous. I was fascinated with the idea, and I agreed."

He nodded, and her agate green eyes stayed on him, narrowing.

"Say it," she said. "What are you thinking?"

He smiled. "You're quick. Did it show that much?"

"Nothing showed. Not approval, not disapproval. That's why I knew you were holding back," Cornelia said. "Go on, say it."

"I'm wondering. No convictions. No principles involved. No judgments. Just a big, exciting game," he said.

"You make me sound so shallow." She laughed.

"Sorry," he said.

"I think I can do it better if I see it as a kind of game, a contest. That way I don't let convictions get in the way, distort my moves, interfere with what I do," she said.

"You might be right. I imagine you use being beautiful, too."

"It's a weapon. It attracts, loosens tongues," she said. "But I don't use it the way you're implying."

"Sorry, again," he said. "It's a pretty damn dangerous game you're into. But you have to know that."

"Yes. That's what fascinates me. I told you, I like dangerous things, dangerous situations, dangerous men," Cornelia Jeffers said, a low laugh in her voice. "They're very hard to find."

The land grew steeper, and the Appalachians rose

up ahead. "What's a dangerous man?" he queried. "One you can't control?"

"That's part of it." She laughed again. "One I can't outwit. One smarter than I am. One who does the unexpected." She let the agate green eyes study him for a long moment. "You could be dangerous," she said, put the buckskin into a canter, and went up a path heavily shaded by bitternut and red mulberry. He followed and saw the long, low cabin. She swung from the buckskin, opened the door, and he followed, seeing the large interior divided into two rooms separated by a heavy curtain on a long rod. A hearth and cordwood occupied one of the rooms; each held a single bed, wooden chairs and throw rugs, and a table completed most of the furnishings. "Now you know where it is, you'll use it instead of the hotel unless there's some emergency. I'll come exploring with you some other time."

"I'll go back with you. I've some things to pick up at the hotel," he said. She stepped outside and he followed her to the rear of the cabin, where he saw a small waterfall.

"I've often come up here just to bathe in the falls. It's wonderful," Cornelia said.

"I could look the other way," he said.

"I don't think you would."

"You have to be more trusting."

"Maybe I'll try, some other time," she said.

"I want to nose around a little," he said, and went to the Ovaro, swung into the saddle, and saw Cornelia follow on her horse. He edged his way into thick tree cover—bitternut, black oak—noting a ground cover of yellow-flowered hop-clover mixed in with pink-blooming cockle. A path opened, and Fargo took it, Cornelia beside him. She saw the wheel tracks at the same time he did, and he heard the excitement catch her voice.

"Look. Maybe we've gotten lucky first crack out," she said. He leaned from the saddle and peered at the tracks, estimating some five or six wagons. "They didn't carry anything but people and household goods," he said. "This is soft ground. They hardly made a dent." She rode alongside him as he moved up the path, pausing as he pointed to a spot on the ground. "They stopped here, made coffee. The ground cover's browned. Our people wouldn't be stopping for anything."

"I see why you were brought in," Cornelia said as they rode on. Finally, he turned when the day began to lengthen.

"I'll get you back and start heavy exploring in the morning," he said. She rode beside him as he turned and moved out of the mountains, passed the cabin, and went east across the rolling terrain of Virginia. When they finally came in sight of Washington, Cornelia reached over, her hand closing on his arm.

"Whatever you find, whatever you need, you get in touch with me. You can leave a note at the cabin if you like. I'll be checking in. You need troops, I'll see that you get them. I'm here for you," she said.

"Sounds good," he commented.

She smiled. "You never know," she said, and stayed with him as they reached his hotel. He saw her eyes grow wide, as did his, when Linda stepped from the lobby.

"Hello," she said, taking in Cornelia with her greeting. Cornelia shot Fargo a glance, a furrow creasing her brow.

He shrugged. "The world's full of surprises," he said.

"I enjoyed the party," Linda said to Cornelia, finding a smile that was more polite than warm.

"I'm glad," Cornelia said, not bothering to smile. She wheeled the buckskin in a circle and shot a glance at Fargo. "Remember everything," she said as she rode away. Fargo dismounted, tethered the Ovaro, and started into the hotel.

"You've been waiting," he said, and she nodded. "How'd you know I'd be here?"

"The desk clerk said you didn't check out."

"I am now. Stopped back to pick up a few things," he said. She went into the room with him and watched as he gathered the clothes he'd left there.

"I came to hear what you have to tell me," Linda said, her tone a challenge.

He debated with himself, heard all the words of caution he'd been given, and wanted to trust Linda. But she was a very angry, upset young woman, perhaps too much so to be closemouthed. He swore silently as he answered. "Don't have anything to tell you," he said.

Her dark blue eyes flashed back. "You mean you don't want to tell me. Be honest," she said. "They tell you not to talk to me?"

"They told me not to talk to anybody."

"Guess I know where I stand."

"Look, give me some more time. Maybe the less you know, the better off you'll be," he tried.

"And I'll never find out who had Kenny killed," she tossed back. "No matter. I know, anyway. Pretty much so."

"What do you know?" He frowned.

"It's got something to do with those little ships," Linda said, and knew his eyes widened in surprise. She tossed in a smile of quiet triumph.

"Where'd you find out about the ships?" he queried.

"A sailor aboard Winslow's frigate is an old friend of Kenny's. He paid me a visit and told me what happened aboard the frigate. I knew it could only have been you," she said, again looking smug. "He also gave me this. Kenny had left it for him," she said, and handed Fargo a small square of notepaper. He looked at the note and read aloud from it.

Dear Richard . . . sorry you're at sea. I stopped by. I'm on the run. They got me into this and I found out something really big. Now I have to hide if I want to stay alive. If you don't hear from me when you get back to shore you'll know they caught up with me. Send this to my sister . . . Kenny.

116

He handed the note back to her, and she put it into a pocket in her skirt. "They caught up to him. We both know that," she said.

He chose words carefully. "I don't know that Kenny's death had anything to do with the ships."

"Maybe it didn't and maybe it did. I'm going to find out. I think it did, somehow, someway," Linda said. "His note makes it plain that he was working for the government. We know Ben Stott hired him, and Ben Stott worked for the government, though you won't say so to me."

"That still doesn't mean they killed him," Fargo said.

"They could be responsible. I'll find out. I'll pin it down," she said stubbornly, casting a sidelong glance at him. "You're not going to help me, are you?" she said.

"I've things to do," he said, half apologetically. "One is not jumping to conclusions like some people I know."

"You jump your way. I'll jump mine," she said tartly, started to turn away, then halted and peered back at him. "That night we had? I'm sorry it happened."

"No, you're not, anymore than I am. You just want more from it than you should," he told her. She strode away, then appeared on the gray mare moments later. "Let me handle it. I'll find out for you," he tried.

She frowned back. "You've been hired, and Cornelia Jeffers is their favorite. None of you is exactly neutral," she said with disdain, put the mare into a canter, and rode away. He thought of following her, trying again to talk sense to her, but realized it'd be a waste of time. The day was sliding away as he trotted through the cobbled streets of the capital. He'd gone only a few blocks when a horse and rider came toward him, and he saw the flame red hair at once.

"Waited for you," Cornelia said. "I want to talk."

"About Linda Corrigan," Fargo grunted.

"Yes," Cornelia said. "Our families go back a ways. But it's your relationship with her that's important."

"I was there when they hunted down her brother."

"I see," Cornelia said, then thought for a moment. "Still, you've been warned not to trust anyone except me. That certainly goes for Linda."

"Why?" Fargo frowned.

"She carries a long-standing grudge against the government," Cornelia said.

"How come?" Fargo questioned with some surprise.

"The government agreed to fund her botany project for eight years. Then Congress changed its mind and backed out of it altogether. She was furious, made a personal appearance before the committee and accused them of betraying her, of having no regard for the environment or their promises. But you know Congress. They'd decided no, and they didn't budge. She promised to make them pay for what they'd done. She wrote letters, buttonholed important people, and got nowhere. She finally got funding from the State of Virginia that has to be renewed every two years. She'd do anything to hurt the government.

She's a very bitter girl, and I think ripe to secessionist influence."

"Still, somebody killed Kenny Corrigan because he found out something," Fargo said.

"Undoubtedly secessionist forces," Cornelia said. "Linda Corrigan has her own axe to grind. Don't trust her."

"Thanks for the background. I'll remember it," Fargo said. "But she's found out things. I wonder how many others have."

"That's why you can't trust anybody," Cornelia said, reaching out to press his arm. "Stay in touch and be careful. I will."

She flicked a rein over the buckskin and rode away, and he watched her go, catching a flash of flame red hair as she passed under a lamplight. He turned the Ovaro and started from the city, riding west across the countryside toward the mountains and the cabin. Linda's words swam back into his mind. *I don't trust the government.* They had a new meaning now. He paused as the Ovaro went up a small hill, and he watched the horse's ears twitch, moving back and forth. Fargo's eyes narrowed, and he waited, listening.

He moved on after a few moments, and the note Linda had shown him returned to his mind. Kenny Corrigan's words had confirmed one thing. He'd been killed for something he'd learned, something so important they had to hunt him down. But it didn't shed any light on the single word he had managed to rasp out with his last few breaths. *Double.* Fargo turned the word in his mind again. Double what? What was he trying to say? What was the double he had discovered? Fargo's thoughts gathered form. Had he come onto someone masquerading, acting as a double? Had he come onto a scheme in which a double would take the place of someone important?

The possibility was staggering. Such a plot could create unimaginable problems, and he felt his excitement growing. Kenny Corrigan's last note and his last word may have combined to unlock a puzzle, perhaps to pinpoint an event still being planned. It was definitely something he ought to run past Cornelia, he decided as the Ovaro moved on through a thick canopy of tall hemlock. When they continued in the tree cover, the horse slowed, blew air, halted, and moved uneasily. He stroked the smooth jet black fur of the horse's neck. "Easy, there," he murmured as he felt his stomach muscles tighten. He didn't need more of a message than the one the Ovaro had given. He wasn't alone. He was being followed, the horse aware even before he had picked it up. He moved the pinto forward at a walk, turning deeper into the forest of hemlock, and the moonlight grew weaker. He swung from the horse, tethered the Ovaro to a low branch, and took small, silent steps until he halted. Hardly breathing, he let his ears depict the dark scene, then heard horses coming closer, moving carefully.

Listening, he counted hoofbeats. One horse first, then another, finally a third—three careful pursuers. They could have attacked him during the past few hours. There had been plenty of chances, spots where an attack could have been made. But they hadn't, which meant they didn't want to kill him, not yet, anyway. They had hung back, content to follow. Their assignment was to trail him, watch, no doubt wait for the morning and see where he went and what he found out, if anything. They probably had orders to strike if he came onto anything. Fargo dropped to one knee as the horses came closer and he finally picked out shadowy shapes. "Shit," he heard the first rider say, his voice a whisper. "We've lost him in this goddamn forest."

Another whispered voice answered. "Let's bed down and pick up his trail in the morning," it said. "We can't find it now." Fargo stayed and watched the three shadowy shapes turn and move back through the forest. He rose, followed on footsteps silent as a puma's, and saw the men find a spot to halt, dismount, and put down their bedrolls. He shrank back and returned to the Ovaro, where he led the horse to a small glen. He paused and considered for a moment. He could go on, but they'd indeed pick up his tracks when morning came. They'd come after him, trailing, watching, waiting. He didn't want that to happen. They had come pursuing him. He'd turn their mission back on them. Stretching out on the leaf-covered ground, he drew sleep around himself, setting his inner alarm clock. With this inner discipline he slept until the final hour of night began to give way to day, when he woke and rose.

Leaving the Ovaro, he stole back to where the three figures were still asleep. The dawn's first gray light pushed forward, and, the Colt in hand, he stepped toward the nearest of the three figures. He had dropped to one knee beside the figure just as the man stirred and sat up rubbing his eyes. The coldness of the gun barrel pressed into his neck, and he snapped his eyes open. "Don't move. Don't do anything stupid," Fargo said quietly.

The man stiffened and swallowed hard, fear gripping his face. "Easy, mister . . . easy," he said. "That could go off."

"Real easy," Fargo agreed, then saw the other two men come awake and sit up. Both reached for their guns. They stared at him. "Put the guns down," Fargo said. Both kept their eyes on him, lowered the guns, but held onto them. "We're going to talk and nobody gets hurt. Who sent you?" Fargo asked.

"Go to hell," one of the men growled.

"Don't be stupid. Nobody has to get hurt. Just tell me who sent you." Fargo repeated. Silence was his only answer. He pressed the Colt harder into the man's neck. "Talk," he demanded. The man's mouth stayed tight as he remained silent, and Fargo felt the first twinge of apprehension. "Come on, they didn't pay you enough to be a hero," Fargo said.

"No, they didn't," the man said, and in surprise Fargo saw the other two bring their guns up again. His apprehension began to balloon. His eyes went to the two other men.

"You'll get him killed. I don't back down," Fargo said. "You're making a big mistake."

"No, you have," one of the men said, and Fargo

swore silently, their answer exploding inside him. They were right. He had made a mistake. He'd taken them as hired guns, and hired guns didn't play heroes. They didn't sacrifice themselves. Only men with commitments did that, and suddenly he realized these were men with a cause, a commitment that rose above self-preservation. He had misjudged them, and it was too late now.

"Shit," he hissed as he saw the two men bring their guns around to fire. His arm shot out, grabbed the man in front of him by the neck, and pulled him back just as the other two fired. Shielding himself behind the man, he felt the man's body shudder as a half-dozen bullets smashed into him. The shuddering stopped, and the man began to sag, but Fargo kept him upright with one arm, brought the Colt up, and fired around the lifeless form in front of him. One of the two men pitched forward as his chest exploded in a shower of red.

Fargo sought out the other man, fired again, but missed as the last man spun and raced for the horses only a few feet away. He leaped onto one, flattened himself in the saddle as Fargo's shot narrowly missed his head, and sent the horse into a gallop. Fargo pushed out from behind the lifeless figure and started to run. The Ovaro would take too long to reach, so he vaulted onto one of the remaining two horses and took off after the fleeing rider. The man heard him coming, turned in the saddle, and fired a wild shot before veering toward a stand of red cedar that rose along a hill. Fargo followed, his horse gaining as the man reached the cedar and plunged into the trees. Fargo followed close behind, heard the horse crashing through underbrush, then suddenly veering left, then right. Fargo cursed. The horse had veered too abruptly, in the way a horse veers when it's suddenly left on its own.

Cursing again, he yanked back on the reins at the same time that he dived from the saddle and felt the shot graze his shoulder as he was in midair. He hit the ground and rolled as another shot plowed into the ground at his elbow. Slamming into a cluster of five-foot-high moth mullein, he let the weeds swallow him up as he whirled and saw another shot come directly across from him. The man had jumped from his horse the minute he'd entered the cedars, a maneuver that had almost worked. But almost wasn't good enough Fargo hissed silently, his lake-blue eyes narrow as he peered at the thicket. He had only to wait another few moments when he saw the low branches move, and he followed the line of them. His target was crawling to his right, moving very slowly, most likely on hands and knees.

Fargo raised the Colt, his eyes following the line of movement where the branches dipped ever so slightly. He waited a moment longer and adjusted his aim, calculating movement and speed. When he fired, he might just as well have had the target in his sights. The man uttered a short cry of gasped pain, and Fargo saw him fall sideways, out from behind the branches and into sight. He fell facedown, tried to rise and fire, only to fall again and lay still. Fargo waited a moment before stepping to the lifeless figure. He turned the man over, searched through his pockets, and found nothing to identify him. But he'd learned perhaps the only important thing. They hadn't been hired killers with no commitment to anything but the dollar. He'd not make the same error again, Fargo promised himself as he walked back to where he'd left the Ovaro and climbed into the saddle.

He rode on east into the fast-rising terrain of the Appalachians, and soon he was slowly moving along the mountainous dips and rises. He searched trails and explored places where there were no trails, searched into hidden passages and others in the open. They had to move their wagons from north to south, if he had calculated correctly. But he could never explore every part of the long, dense sweep of the mountains. However, there was a way, he decided, and he searched east to west, certain he'd eventually spot where the wagons crossed direction with him. But even that was a formidable task. The mountain plant growth was quick to cover every inch of land with almost gleeful abandon as the towering ash, box elder, sycamore, and shagbark hickory looked down approvingly. By the end of the day he had found some wheel tracks, but none that fitted what he searched to see.

He had just pushed into the open from a long, cedar-covered passage when he saw the gray mare and its rider standing in front of him. "What are you doing here?" he asked, frowning.

"I've been on the high ridge," Linda said.

"Watching me, sneaking after me," Fargo said, and dismounted.

"It's a free country. I can go wherever I want," she said defensively.

"Dammit, girl, this is no Easter egg hunt. You can cause real trouble, to say nothing of getting in my way," Fargo threw back.

"Then tell me what it's all about," she insisted adamantly.

"Can't," he said.

"Then I'll keep looking for the connection," she said.

"What connection?" He frowned.

"Between what you're looking for and why Kenny was killed."

He speared her with a hard glance, but she threw it back. "I don't know that there is a connection," he said in honesty. Maybe there was, and maybe there really wasn't. Maybe Kenny's knowledge had other roots. He'd no way of knowing yet. He couldn't say more. Couldn't and wouldn't.

"You could be holding back," she said, the remark accusing, yet pleading.

"Holding back? That's your department," he said.

Her eyes grew wary at once. "Meaning what?"

"Meaning that the government refused to fund your project. You never mentioned that. Why not?" Fargo tossed at her.

"I was afraid you'd jump to the wrong conclusions, just the way you're doing now," Linda said.

"Wrong conclusions? I think they're the right

126

ones," he said. "You want your own grudges confirmed. You're convinced the government is responsible for Kenny's death. You've said as much. It gives you an excuse to get back at them."

"You think I'm wrong? Then help me find out," she said.

"I will, when and if it comes my way. Meanwhile, you back off. Don't get in the way," he said.

"That's not good enough," she said.

"It's all I'll give you," he said.

"Then I keep looking on my own. There's a connection. I know it," Linda said, her lips tightening.

"I don't like being spied on," Fargo said, warning in his voice.

"You won't mind if I find something to help you," she returned airily, pulled the mare around, and rode away. He let her go in the last of the daylight and swore softly. Perhaps he was handling her the wrong way, he pondered as he slowly moved downhill. She had already discovered the fact about the ships. She was too smart not to have put the rest together. He found a spot between two cedars and set out his bedroll as he continued to think about Linda. She knew he searched for tracks, though she didn't know the details. Maybe bringing her partly in with him would keep her from being a source of trouble and let him keep an eye on her. The thought grew more appealing as he stretched out in the warm night. Maybe he could get her to back off in time, he mused. But he'd keep the cabin from her, he decided. He'd not compromise Cornelia's safe house. He went to sleep with his mind made up, then slept soundly until the morning woke him.

He rose, washed, and rode the Ovaro in a wide circle that brought him up at the rear part of the high ridge. Linda didn't hear him until he was but a few yards from her. She had her shirt in hand, was just beginning to put it on, and he let himself enjoy the upturned, saucy breasts, as beautifully pert as he remembered. "Real nice," he said softly, and she spun, both high-pointed breasts bouncing in unison.

"Dammit, Fargo," she hissed, then pulled the shirt on. "Sneaking up on people your latest thing?"

"Thought I'd save you looking for me," he said blandly as she tucked the shirt into her Levi's, her face still angry. "Been thinking that you might as well ride along as follow."

She frowned and gave him a suspicious glance. "That's a sudden change of heart. Why?"

"Thought about it, slept on it. Maybe I've been too hard-nosed with you, and I can use help. You follow orders, and I'll tell you what I know and what I find out," Fargo said.

"It's a deal," Linda said instantly. "You first."

"You know about the small cutters. They're being brought in through the mountains before taken to a place to launch them," he said.

"Is that what Kenny found out?" Linda asked.

"I don't know. Maybe it is, but I'm convinced that's the way they're being brought in. I've got to find the trail, the wagon tracks. Then maybe I can find out the rest. Maybe that is the connection with Kenny's death." He waited, confident it had been enough for her. Her eyes swept the towering denseness of the mountains.

"How can they get wagons big enough to carry the ships through these mountains?" she asked.

"Been asking that myself. Somehow, they're doing it. Maybe there are hidden passages big enough. That's why finding the tracks is everything." She nodded, accepting his answer. "We'll separate now. You go west. I'm going east in case they're going through the low valleys," he said.

"If I find tracks?" Linda asked.

"Follow them, remember where you found them. We'll meet back here at the end of the day. Good luck," he said. She nodded, took the gray mare, and rode away and was quickly swallowed up in the mountain denseness. He turned and sent the Ovaro downward, exploring as he made his way down narrow trails. When he came in sight of the cabin, he put the Ovaro into a fast canter when he saw the buckskin outside. Cornelia came out as he skidded to a stop, flame red hair glinting in the morning sun, a green shirt that almost matched her eyes as it clung to the deep breasts. "Glad you're here. I came to leave you a note," he said.

"I just left you one telling you I'd be back tomorrow," Cornelia said. "You find something?"

"No tracks yet, but something else, something you should know," he said, and went into the cabin with her. She listened with a deepening frown as he told her about Kenny Corrigan's last note and his last word. The agate green eyes stared at him when he finished.

"Good God, a double," she murmured, almost in shock.

"That's the only meaning I can get out of it," Fargo said.

"I'm sure you're right. There's no other way to interpret it," Cornelia agreed. "If they brought in a double for anyone important, it could create God knows how much trouble. Imagine a double for Captain Winslow, Chief of Staff Evans, John Nicolay. My God, the thought's staggering."

"That's why I thought I'd best get this to you," Fargo said.

"Good God, yes. I'll go back and start immediate countermoves. Did you tell Linda what you put together?" Cornelia asked.

"No, decided the fewer people know about this the better."

"Yes. Let's keep it that way."

"Besides, it still doesn't nail down who killed Kenny, and that's what she wants to find out," Fargo said.

"You've done brilliantly, Fargo. You figured out what Kenny Corrigan was trying to say with his last word, and you've given us time to counter their insidious plans," Cornelia said. Her arms rose, encircled his neck, and he felt her lips on his, soft and warm, a slight quiver in their touch. Her full, deep breasts came against his chest, beautifully soft, and then she pulled away. "Special work deserves special thanks," she said, a tiny glint in the agate green eyes.

"I'll remember that. Gives me another reason for finding tracks," Fargo said.

"I'll visit again," she said, and he gave her a hand up onto the buckskin. She took the saddle with one unbroken motion, and he decided there was nothing Cornelia Jeffers did that wasn't both graceful and striking. She blew a kiss as she rode away, and he turned the pinto up into the high mountains. He spent the rest of the day searching the terrain, but found only two small sets of tracks that could only have been made by a pair of buckboards and was back on the high ridge as the sun dipped behind the distant peaks. Linda appeared soon after, her face unhappy and tired.

"Nothing," she said crossly.

"They're someplace. We keep looking," he said.

"Your hidden passages?" she slid at him.

"Probably. I'm sure they exist, too," he said, then dismounted and unsaddled the pinto. "This is as good a spot to bed down as any," he said.

She swung from the gray mare and set her blanket down a few yards from him. When dark fell, she changed before the moon rose high enough to light the mountains and sat cross-legged in the short, knee-length blue nightdress. She had her own cold strips of beef jerky, and Fargo ate of his supply. "Going to stay way over there?" he asked when they finished the meal.

"Yes," she said.

"Thought we'd made a truce," he said.

"A truce isn't a peace pact," Linda sniffed. "While I was searching, I got to thinking that you really didn't tell me a hell of a lot." He half smiled as he grudgingly admired her sharp tenacity. "There's more you haven't said," she muttered.

"You want to back out searching for me?" he asked.

"No, but I'm not just searching for you. I'm searching for myself."

"Being a scientist again, keeping things separate," he pushed at her.

"That's right, and I've decided one thing. No matter why Kenny was killed, or who did it, the government put his life on the line. They're responsible for that and maybe more. They deserve to pay for that much."

"If you've decided that, leave it there. Go home. Stop risking your neck," Fargo said.

"Oh, no. I want that final truth. I won't be satisfied till I have that," she said.

"You call it that final truth. Be honest. It's revenge you want," he said.

"It's justice for Kenny," she returned angrily, then turned her back to him with a flounce and pulled the blanket around herself. He undressed and let sleep come to him until the morning dawned. He woke first, used his canteen to wash, and was dressed when Linda sat up.

"I'll find us some breakfast," he said, then disappeared into the green forests. She was dressed when he returned, his hat filled with pawpaws and berries, which she ate with hungry enjoyment.

"Never had these berries before," she said, savoring the sweet-sour taste of one on her tongue.

"Mooseberries," he told her. "Some folks call them highbush cranberries." When they'd breakfasted, he led the way north along a deep ridge dense with white ash. He rode almost a half mile from her, and when the day ended, neither had found any wagon tracks.

"No second thoughts?" Linda asked before they slept in the dark of the night.

"Only about these damn mountains that swallow everything up," he said crossly. "But that's not the worst of it."

"What is? Me sleeping way over here?" she asked tartly.

"Don't be a smart-ass," he growled.

"What's the worst of it?" she pressed.

"Knowing that there's something going on up here in these mountains and we can't get a lead," he said, frustration evident in his voice.

"You really believe that?" she said.

"I know it, feel it inside me," Fargo said, silently cursing the instincts he could neither deny nor define.

8

The dapper figure moved gracefully as he took the
cup of coffee from his valet, who instantly disappeared with practiced ease. General Pierre Gustave
Toutant Beauregard sipped from the lip of the delicate, fine English bone china cup, drew in a deep
breath, and savored the delicious aroma of the High
Mountain coffee he had specially shipped from Ja-
maica. He smiled at his visitor, who was all but invisible in the huge chair with the enveloping William and
Mary arms.

"I understand the problem," the dapper general
said, and smiled confidently. "But it will be handled
by good, solid military tactics."

"Military tactics?" His visitor frowned.

"Yes, by the oldest and still most reliable of
all . . . the diversions," General Beauregard said. "Let
me explain something to you. A proper diversionary
maneuver is not merely setting out a decoy to deceive
your enemy. A proper diversion should lure him into
committing a costly, preferably irretrievable error.
This is what I will do." He paused and took another

sip of coffee. "They are stretched thin now, trying to cover too many places, prepare for too many eventualities. I shall make them even thinner by wiping out a good part of them."

"What about this Trailsman?" his visitor asked.

"I expect he will be wiped out with the others. You could call it a case of killing numerous birds with one stone," the general said. "Have you told Senator Slidell or Congressman Murray?"

"Yes. They said to put it in your lap."

"Of course. This is exactly why I was brought in. By the way, word has it that I'm to be given command of the regiment at Charleston."

"Congratulations."

"Of course, this has to wait for events to move further along," the general said.

"Then you'll write me."

"Soon, very soon. I anticipated a problem such as this and had my plans ready, my men waiting."

"One thing more. As you've heard, the Trailsman doesn't lure easily. Every attempt to kill him has failed."

The general's smile was almost chiding. "As we say back in Louisiana, I never saw a fox that could resist a hen house," he said.

9

Two more days had passed, and they had found only the tracks of an isolated buckboard, assorted footprints, some of them barefoot, and the marks of beaver traps that had been dragged by their owners. But now something really ominous had appeared, and Fargo grimaced as he looked up at the sky of grayness growing deeper by the minute. He threw a glance at Linda. "Yes, I see it," she said.

"It's going to be a bad one, plenty of wind and rain," Fargo said. "You know what these storms can be like up here in the mountains. Hell, you live up here."

"Yes, I've been through enough of them," she said.

"But in a house, with protection, not out here in the open," he said. "It's flash floods and whole forests uprooted out here, danger coming from everywhere. I want you to ride down to the flatland and sit it out someplace down there."

"What about you?" She frowned, and he swore inwardly. He wanted to take her to the protection of the cabin, but he couldn't risk compromising Cornelia's safe house. Feeling guilty and deceitful, he tried to evade a direct answer.

"I'll be all right," he said.

Her frown deepened at him. "That's no answer. You're playing games again," she said, her acute instincts flaring up instantly.

"I'm not. Just get going while you can," he said.

"No. I'll be all right," she said.

"Now who's playing games?" he returned.

"Two can play at that." She turned the mare and rode away at a trot.

"Don't be dumb. Go down. Get out of the mountains," he called after her.

"Same to you," she flung back without turning.

He cursed the damn stubbornness of her. "See you here when it's over," he called, but she didn't turn and didn't answer. He wheeled the Ovaro and rode east, hoping she really did have a place to go, as he disliked the role in which he found himself. The gray sky grew grayer, and the wind started to rustle the tops of the trees. By the time he reached the cabin, the day was nearly at an end and the rain had begun. He went into the cabin, rummaged through both rooms, and found a large piece of tarpaulin that he dragged outside and, using his lariat, rigged up a lean-to for the Ovaro. He tied it tight to four trees and tested it, satisfied that it'd keep the worst of the rain from the horse.

Fargo had stretched out on one of the beds when the first fury of the storm struck. He lay awake and listened to the storm quickly grow in intensity, wind and rain becoming torrential. But it was not the storm that kept him awake. He'd slept through many a storm. It was short-cropped, dark blond hair and dark blue eyes that kept him awake, a pert face that accused at the same time that it appealed. Questions swirled around him, questions he was not accustomed to facing. Had he done the right thing? Should he have taken her with him? But had he any right to disregard the warnings, instructions, and advice he had been given? The questions refused to let him do more than catnap until morning came and the storm continued in its fury. He finally fell asleep, then woke late in the day to see the rain still drenching the land. He chewed on some cold beef strips, brewed coffee on the hearth, and lay down again, forcing himself not to think about Linda and his decisions.

He slept when the night grew late and woke to a new day and the sound of songbirds. Sun flooded through the cabin window, and he gazed out at forests still glistening green and wet with raindrops unwilling to evaporate. He went outside and let the Ovaro loose where it could move into the hot sun and dry off. The morning sun had risen higher toward the noon sky when he rode from the cabin. The air still smelled of wetness, and the chorus frogs were out in full force, reveling in the moist forests. He felt the Ovaro's hooves sinking into the softness of ground soaked deep and made his way to the high ridge. When he reached it, he was surprised at the rush of relief that swept through him when he saw the gray mare and the figure beside it.

"Hello," he said. "You don't look any the worse for wear, I'm glad to see."

"I told you I'd be all right," Linda said coolly.

"I was worried about you," he said.

"Not enough to take me with you," she sniffed, and he was glad there was more bite than hurt in her tone. She held him with a slightly superior stare. "They came," she said, making it sound like an announcement. He frowned at her. "Wagons. During the storm," she said.

"Goddamn," he exploded. "You see them?"

"No," she said.

"You saw tracks," he said.

"Somebody else did and told me," Linda said. "They went along the low valley this side of the Blue Ridge."

"Can you show me?" he asked, excitement spiraling through him.

"Yes," she said, and climbed onto the mare as he swung in beside her. "You owe me after this. No more holding back, not anything," she said.

"A deal," he agreed, and rode beside her through narrow passages where hemlock and black oak leaned in from both sides. They rode through one heavily forested passage after another until suddenly he saw the tracks that came down from high ground to stretch out along a deep cut. They were clear and deep where they had traveled over the rain-soaked ground. He dismounted and moved on foot to study them more closely. He saw where they overlapped and counted at least eight wagons. The excitement that had caught hold of him grew less intense, and Linda saw the furrow his brow.

"What is it?" she questioned.

"These aren't buckboard tracks, but they're not the kind of big wagons I expected," he said. "I figure they're mountain wagons at best."

"It's still them. It can't be anybody else," she said.

"I guess not," he agreed as he climbed back onto his horse. "Let's track." Linda stayed close as he began to follow the wheel tracks, saw them lead downward, stay mostly in narrow passages, but still make their way downward. They led in the right direction. They were what he'd come to find. They plainly headed down out of the mountains. It all fit, and he wished he could recapture the first moment of excitement he'd felt. They were following the wheel tracks that curved out of the end of a low valley when Linda questioned him.

"What's the matter?" she asked.

"Nothing. Why?"

"Been watching your face. All you're doing is frowning," she said, and he grimaced at her acuity.

"Sorry," he said. "I'm always extra cautious." He shot a glance at her and saw her accept the answer without really accepting it. Perhaps he was simply being overly cautious, he told himself, and tried to put away the undefined, nagging something that refused to be put aside. But as dusk began to descend and the wagon tracks left the last low valley to stretch eastward across the flat land, he felt the excitement beginning again. The trail followed pretty much as he expected it would, coming down from the mountains to move across the flat land.

"You know where we are?" he asked Linda.

"Swift Run Gap ought to be just south of us," she said.

"That means the beginning of the Rapidan is just below us," he said, feeling a new surge of excitement. Everything was beginning to fit tighter. Night descended as the tracks stretched over a low hill, downward on the other side and then to another low rise. They had gone another few miles and the moon had risen high enough to show the deep tracks go over the small rise when he suddenly pulled to a halt. He touched Linda's arm, and she stopped as Fargo inclined his head to one side, listening, letting his wild-creature hearing sort out sounds.

"I don't hear anything," Linda said.

"I do. Voices. Knives scraped against tin plates. The lid of a coffeepot," Fargo whispered, and swung from the pinto, letting the reins drop to the ground. Linda dismounted, and he glanced at the mare.

"She'll stay," Linda said. He started forward, heard Linda beside him, and halted.

"Take off your shoes. You're not quiet enough with them on," he said. She slid her shoes off and carried them as he started forward again over the low rise. Reaching the top, he dropped down onto his stomach and pulled Linda with him. A huge warehouse rose up at the bottom of the rise, its size and shape marking it at once as a tobacco drying shed. But in front of this tobacco holding warehouse Fargo saw at least fifty armed guards, each with a rifle. A half dozen more men dished food from skillets while others collected tin plates from those finished with their meal.

"Bull's-eye," Linda whispered. "You've found them. The ships are inside that warehouse."

"Sure seems so," Fargo said.

"Of course they are. There wouldn't be fifty armed guards around a tobacco drying warehouse."

"It's not likely," he agreed.

"It's more than not likely. What are you so damn reluctant for?" she thrust at him.

"I don't know. Something keeps nagging at me, but I can't pin it down," Fargo said.

"Stop being ridiculous. Of course this is it," Linda said.

"It sure seems so," he conceded. "That's a good-sized force at that warehouse, which means I'm going to need help, a lot of it. I'm going to get it. Meanwhile, they might send out patrols during the night. I don't want you here."

"I don't want to be here," she said. "I'll go back into the mountains."

"Good. Let's go," he said, and began to back down the low rise, Linda alongside him, until they reached the horses. He paused beside her on the Ovaro. "Where'll I find you?" he asked.

"The high ridge, same place. You've done your job. Let the others do the fighting," she said, wheeled the mare, and rode away. He put the Ovaro into a gallop and began to race across the Virginia countryside toward Washington. He stopped twice

142

to rest the horse, then resumed the ride, and the first pink light of dawn tinged the sky as he reached the capital. The sun was up when he halted at the mansion, pounded at the door, and a servant answered. He pushed his way past. "Tell Miss Jeffers she has a visitor," he said.

"I have it, Robert," the voice said, and Fargo turned to see Cornelia, flame red hair flowing around her as though it were a fiery halo, a pale blue nightgown clinging to every sumptuous curve of her body. "This must be important," she said to Fargo and motioned him into a small study. He followed her and wondered if there was a time when she didn't look stunningly beautiful. She turned and faced him inside the study after closing the door. He had to force his eyes from the swell of her breasts, which pushed up over the neckline of the nightgown.

"It looks like we've found the ships," he said, and quickly told her what he'd tracked down.

"I'd say there's no question about it. What great news," Cornelia said excitedly. "You've come to get a support force."

"A hundred men at least." He nodded.

"How soon?" she asked.

"Now. Fast as you can. I want to get back there by midnight. They could be getting ready to move out down to the Rapidan," Fargo said.

"I'll dress and get right at it. I'll still need a couple of hours," Cornelia said, and peered at him. "You've been riding all night. Why don't you get some rest while I make my contacts?"

"That sounds good," he said, and she took his arm as she led him to a guest room where a large four-poster beckoned invitingly.

"See to my horse, food, and a rub-down," Fargo said.

"It's done," she said, then paused. "You never told me how you found their tracks. You just come onto them?"

"Somebody told me about them," he said. "I went looking for them and found them."

"Get some rest. I'll wake you when I get back," she said, giving him a quick hug. "This is really exciting. You've done wonderfully, just wonderfully." He nodded and wondered why he couldn't muster the same excitement, why something still pulled at him. When she hurried from the room, he pulled off outer clothes and lay atop the bed, slept in minutes, and woke only when he heard the door being opened. Cornelia came in wearing a black shirt and black jodhpurs, a striking contrast to her flame red hair. She paused for a moment, her eyes moving across the muscled beauty of his torso as he started to pull on clothes. "There are a hundred and twenty-five federal troops waiting outside, from the Seventh Cavalry stationed here in Washington," Cornelia said.

"That ought to do it," Fargo said.

"I'm going with you," she said as he finished dressing.

He looked unhappy. "This won't be any picnic."

"All the more reason. I want to be able to give a personal report to the president," she said. He

144

shrugged and followed her from the house, then halted as his eyes swept the horses and troopers lined up in columns of eight. An officer came forward to meet him. "Captain Stanton," Cornelia said. "I've briefed the captain on the situation."

"Seems pretty simple to me, Fargo. You take us there, and we'll wipe them out," the captain said, a man with a career soldier's air to him.

"Seems so," Fargo said. "I'll pin it down when we get closer." He swung onto the Ovaro, and Cornelia came alongside him as he began to ride due west.

"What'd that mean?" she questioned at once.

"I'm not sure," he admitted. "Something bothers me."

"What?"

"I don't know. Something. Maybe I'm being too careful," he said. "I'll think more on it as we ride." She nodded and fell silent as he set a steady pace to the drumbeat sound of the horses behind him. The day had begun to slide toward its end when the distant mountains came into view and Cornelia's voice found him.

"Done your thinking?" she asked.

He nodded, not happily. He'd searched his thoughts as they rode, and the undefined had taken on substance. "Little things," he said to her. "Always pay attention to little things. Learned that long ago."

"Such as?" she questioned.

"They've been so careful up to now. No tracks, nothing for anyone to pick up, sneaking through the mountain passages. Why'd they go through the storm?" he asked.

"The storm was a cover, an ideal one, it seems to me," Cornelia said.

"One thing more that's not what it seems. I'm sure they've been moving at night, but there's a moon by night. The mountains were pitch black during that storm. Moving wagons through the storm was taking a hell of a risk. Zero visibility, ground that gives way under a wagon or horses, the chances of getting stuck and never getting free, and, of course, doing just what they did, leaving deep, clear tracks. "Why?" he asked again. "Why didn't they wait for another night, after the storm passed?"

"Maybe they have a schedule to follow?" Cornelia suggested.

"No schedule can be that tight in this kind of an operation," Fargo said.

"You know what I think, Fargo?" Cornelia thrust at him. "I think you just can't believe you've found them this soon."

He allowed a wry snort. "Maybe, but I want another look," he said, and led the troops in a long circle as night descended. They rode another three hours, the moon close to the midnight sky, when he neared the first of the two rises before the warehouse. He drew to a halt, dismounted, and Captain Stanton rode up to him. "They're just over the next rise," Fargo said. "Keep your men here. They'll be heard if they ride any closer."

"Yes," the captain said as he swung from his mount.

"I'm going closer for another look," Fargo said.

"I'll go along. I want to have a look before we go charging in," Stanton said.

"I'm coming," Cornelia said. She met Fargo's dubious gaze. "Have you forgotten my role in all this?" she asked softly.

"No, but I think you're too beautiful to get shot," he said.

"Gallantry and charm. Delightful. But I'm still coming along," she said.

"I'll see that Miss Jeffers is at the rear when we charge," the captain said, Cornelia's half shrug consent. Fargo started forward on foot, crossed the top of the second rise, and dropped to his stomach to gaze at the huge warehouse. Cornelia came beside him, Captain Stanton at his other side. Fargo's eyes swept the site and saw the guards still fronting the huge shed, still at least fifty of them. Moreover, they were all alert.

"Dammit, I'd hoped for only a dozen sentries awake," he muttered. "I want a look inside that warehouse."

"Isn't it obvious, Fargo? They wouldn't have all these men guarding a tobacco drying shed," Cornelia said.

"I still want a look inside. Maybe there's something else going on we don't have any idea about," Fargo said.

147

"I suppose that's some sort of remote possibility, but I'm sure it's the ships," she said.

"You two stay here. Give me twenty minutes."

"You're mad, Fargo. A snake couldn't sneak through that bunch," Stanton said.

"There's a stand of hackberry a dozen feet from the back side," Fargo said. "I'll go that way."

"You're not back in twenty minutes my men will be charging," Stanton said. Fargo nodded, left them, and keeping to a crawl, moved sideways to a thin line of trees, where he stayed as he slid forward past the side of the warehouse. His lips drew back as he saw a line of guards covering the side of the shed, but he crawled forward again and reached the rear of the structure.

"Damn," he hissed when he saw the row of guards across the back of the shed. But as he peered hard at them, he saw that they weren't as alert as the obviously main crew at the front of the building. Half leaned back against the building wall, their eyes closed, he noted. He'd come this far and was of no mind to turn back unless he had to, he decided. Reaching down to his calf, he brought the thin, double-edged throwing knife from its holster. Clutching it in his right hand, he began to crawl from the treeline into the open. He inched his way forward, eyes sweeping the guards as he did. The ones awake stared past him toward the trees, and he continued to crawl, each movement snail-like, and he headed toward two guards asleep at the corner. He finally neared them, casting a glance at the others every other second, grateful for the dark shadow cast by the height of the big tobacco shed.

As he drew closer, he saw the outlines of a narrow door in the shed, perhaps another dozen feet on. He shifted his body and went toward it, even though he'd have to pass almost in front of the two sleeping guards. He inched on, passed the first of the two men, then was in front of the second when he heard the man snap awake, a grunt coming from him. Fargo froze in place, his eyes lifting up to the man, and he held his breath as the man blinked and peered forward into the darkness and the trees. He didn't glance down to the figure practically at his feet, grunted again, leaned back against the shed, and closed his eyes.

Slowly, Fargo let a trickle of breath escape his lips, remained motionless, and trained his eyes on the other guards. They were focused into the distance, none aware of the shape right in front of them. Again, Fargo began to inch forward, almost abreast of the narrow door when his luck exploded and he heard shouts of surprise and dismay. He'd been discovered. "Shit," he swore as he rolled and came up on one knee to see the man staring at him, then start to run at him, raising his rifle. Others were springing into action behind the man, and Fargo dived forward at the figure in front of him. The man tried to bring his rifle up, but Fargo slashed with the blade, a half uppercut, half hook, and the man flew backward with a roar of pain, red drops flying into the air from his neck and chin.

He fell, and Fargo saw the others coming toward him, raising rifles. He tucked the throwing knife into his belt as he yanked the Colt from its holster. His first two shots struck the nearest two figures, and they went down together, as if pulled by the same rope. Fargo dived and rolled along the ground as a cluster of rifle shots erupted, all missing, all wide of the mark. He leaped up, then ran in a darting criss-cross pattern for the trees as more shots missed. He reached the hackberry as bullets slammed into the trees, ran a dozen feet, turned, and saw the guards running after him. He fired again, two more shots, and two figures fell, one stumbling over the other. Turning, he raced into the trees, ran for another dozen feet, and dropped to one knee.

The gunfire had alerted everyone now, he knew, but there was no rush of guards from the other side of the big shed. They had left it to the guards at the rear, and Fargo saw the figures come into the trees and spread out to search for him. He stayed still as a rock. By now the other guards weren't the only ones to have heard the shots, and he hoped he'd bought enough time to save his neck. The figures moving through the trees came toward him, still spreading out, and he counted ten. Distant shouts and com-mands echoed from the front of the shed, and Fargo stayed in place, letting the figures move closer.

Slowly, he raised the Colt and picked out two fig-ures at the right. His finger was on the trigger when shouts echoed through the night, and then he heard the unmistakable sound of hoofbeats thundering across the ground in an all-out charge. He saw the figures in front of him halt, spin, and run out of the forest toward the big shed. A volley of gunshots exploded in the night, then another volley as Fargo ran from the trees. Captain Stanton had reached the shed, and his troopers were engaged in a pitched battle. Fargo ran along the side of the shed, reached the front of it, and saw the guards falling back in disarray at the full brunt of the attack, at least twenty already on the ground. But he saw blue-coated uniforms prostrate on the soil also, and he ran forward and brought down two guards as he fired. Stanton's men had reached the wide doors of the shed, and a half dozen leaped from their horses, took hold of the doors, and pulled them open.

A thunderous explosion of gunfire blasted from the opened doors, and Fargo heard himself cursing as he saw the rifle-carrying figures racing out of the shed. At least fifty, perhaps more, he guessed. But the concentrated fire and surprise of their attack wrought havoc among Stanton's troops as dozens fell from their horses. He heard Stanton shouting commands over the din of rifle fire and shouts, trying to rally his units, as the attackers continued to pour out of the shed, firing volley after volley. Fargo dropped to one knee, aimed, and brought down three more of the attackers, then dropped low to avoid an answering fusillade of shots. The captain had rallied at least some of his troops, Fargo saw, and they had collected themselves enough to fight back from formation. They were doing real damage to the attackers, he saw, but it had become a terrible carnage. Suddenly, Fargo saw what was left of the attackers begin to run. They fled the scene into the trees behind the warehouse.

"Stand back," he heard the captain call, and he nodded in agreement. There was no point in pursuit and perhaps the danger of another trap somewhere. Fargo rose, holstered the Colt, and surveyed the ground covered with slain figures. He strode to the shed and stepped inside, his lips a thin line as rage boiled within at what he saw. Emptiness, vast emptiness. The warehouse held nothing but the drying racks suspended from the ceiling.

"Dammit," he muttered as his eyes moved across the floor and saw nothing, not even a piece of rope. The warehouse had never held the ships. Never. The fact burned into him—searing, mocking, taunting. The gunfire had stopped, and he heard footsteps behind him, then turned to see Captain Stanton, his face drained of color.

"The bastards. Most of my troop's gone," the captain said hoarsely. "They were waiting for us."

Fargo nodded and felt sick inside himself. Another figure appeared in the doorway, flame red hair framing the feature-perfect face. He stared at her, letting her see the bitterness in his face. "You were right," she said. "You suspected something."

"Not this," he bit out as she took his arm.

"You're alive—that's important," Cornelia said.

"I was set up, sent on a wild-goose chase with an ambush waiting. Meanwhile, they were moving the ships through another route," Fargo said, and swore silently at himself. He hadn't listened to those warning instincts that were always so right. He'd wanted to believe he had found the ships, and now too many had paid the price.

Cornelia cast a quizzical glance at him. "You said somebody put you onto the tracks. Could that have been Linda Corrigan?" she asked, and he felt surprise flood his face.

"How'd you know?" he questioned.

"She's been searching and snooping up into the mountains. We have our sources, and she's been pretty open about it," Cornelia said. "That might explain a lot."

He frowned back. "What are you saying?"

"She has her grudge against the government, and she holds the government at least partly responsible for Kenny's death. She's made no secret about that. This could spell revenge."

Fargo stared at Cornelia as he wrestled with the whirlwind of thoughts that spiraled through him. "She never organized this," he said. "This took planning, experience, coordination."

"No, she didn't. But she could have cooperated. All she had to do was throw you the bait and let the rest follow."

He continued to stare at Cornelia, her words churning inside him, beyond believing yet not at all beyond believing, impossible yet very possible. He swore silently as he answered. "I'll find out. That's a promise." He started to turn away. "Now I'm going back. I've tracks to find, the right ones."

"I'll stay to help Captain Stanton. A lot of people will be descending with a lot of questions, state officials, national officials, town officials. I can answer some of what they'll be asking and give them the people to reach," Cornelia said.

"No wonder they have the confidence they do in you at the top," Fargo said.

Her hand reached out and pressed his arm. "It wasn't your doing. Don't go blaming yourself."

"I asked myself questions and didn't listen. There's blame enough in that," he said tightly.

"I'll be visiting," she called after him as he left her, went outside, and searched till he found the Ovaro. He rode slowly, back toward the unyielding Appalachians and Cornelia's words churned in his mind. Linda's remarks returned to him.

It's them. It can't be anybody else.

Bull's-eye. You've found them. The ships are inside that warehouse.

There wouldn't be fifty armed guards around a tobacco drying warehouse.

Stop being ridiculous. Of course this is it.

He turned the words over and over in his mind—words of support, encouragement, agreement. Had she simply been as fooled as he was? Or had they all been words of betrayal, words wrapped in a different motivation? He cursed softly as he recalled that Cornelia had uttered almost the same words. Only hers were not touched with hatred, revenge, and distrust.

The pinto began the climb into the mountain terrain, and Fargo made a promise to himself. He'd find out about words and reasons, innocence or betrayal. Sooner or later, he'd find out, just as he'd find the goddamn tracks.

10

He slept a few hours in the cabin and was in the saddle again before dawn, reaching the high ridge soon after the sun came up. He sat in a clump of sunflowers, and the morning drifted toward noon when the gray mare pushed through the trees. Linda, wearing a tan vest over a white shirt, dismounted, her face unsmiling. She faced him, hands on her hips. "I'm glad you came through it," she said.

"Is that all you can say?" Fargo asked.

"Thought you'd like hearing that."

"How'd you learn about it?" he questioned, his face stern.

"I wasn't that far away. Besides, there was plenty of talk afterward."

He rose to his feet, his face set. "It was a setup, a diversion, the tracks, the route, the guards, the warehouse, all of it, especially the tracks," he said.

She saw that his lake-blue eyes were cold as ice floes as they bored into her. Her eyes grew narrow as she peered back. "You're blaming me, aren't you?"

He shrugged. "You led me to the tracks," he said.

"That implicates me? You've no cause to say that," Linda protested.

"I'm not big on coincidences and grudges," he said.

"That's rotten, real rotten. You were fooled. So was I."

He leveled a skeptical glance at her. "You said somebody pointed the tracks out to you."

"That's right," she snapped.

"Who?"

"Somebody. An old friend, a lot of old friends."

"Not good enough. Words are cheap. Show me. Give me some proof if you want me to believe you," Fargo said.

"Bastard," Linda flung at him. He shrugged, unmoved. "Follow me," she hissed, and pulled herself onto the mare. He followed as she rode down the far side of the ridge and into a dense mountain fastness. She pushed through heavy stands of red mulberry, hemlock, and black walnut, then moved into a passage too narrow for more than one horse at a time. The pass twisted and turned, surrounded by dense forests, and finally he saw her disappear around a sharp curve. He followed, speeding the horse forward around the curve, and reared back almost in shock, certainly in surprise.

A wide, deep cleared part of the dense forest opened up before him, as if a little community had been magically transported into the inner depths of the forest. He saw shacks that seemed to be hanging on hillsides, tar paper huts shouldering pig pens, more ramshackle dwellings in a half circle behind big, open iron kettles that were bubbling and steaming with cooking aromas. Linda had dismounted and halted in front of some of the figures that seemed frozen in place. Fargo took in large, beefy men, most in overalls, some only in trousers, most wearing full beards and long hair. Women in frayed, worn dresses looked at him from small knots, their faces weathered, hair more tangled than combed, yet somehow many retaining a wild handsomeness. Nearly naked children watched from off to one side.

"These are my friends, the Timbersville Mountain people," Linda said.

"This where you stayed during the storm?" he asked.

She nodded. "Remember, I told you how my pa brought me with him when he went hunting? This is where we came," Linda said, and half turning to the others, gestured to Fargo. "This is Skye Fargo. He's come all the way from the Western territories," she said. She motioned with one hand as she spoke to Fargo. "That's Zeke Cole over there, Rebecca, Sarah and, Hedda Cole," she said, then indicated another group of undershirted men and raggedy women. "Ebenezer Crabble, Elwood Crabble, Mary, Sally, Hilda, and Inge Crabble. The Cole cousins are over there by the big shack, the Dorrances by the tar paper house."

"Everybody related?" Fargo asked.

"More or less," Linda said. His eyes swept the scene again, pausing at the rifles that leaned against every shack. He saw some old Walken plains rifles, a few carbines the army had stopped using years ago, and a collection of long-barreled varmint rifles. All were old and unwieldy, yet still deadly accurate in the hands of expert marksmen, and he had no doubt that these mountain men were that. A few more figures sauntered out of the foliage at the rear of the cleared land, some younger women, two with babies in their arms. Linda stepped forward, her eyes sweeping the thick walls of surrounding oaks. "Joey, get out here right now," she called, then waited. Fargo caught the movement in the trees and saw a figure burst into view, swinging out of the trees on a long rope to drop lightly to the ground next to Linda.

He stared at a young girl, jet black hair and eyes almost as black, a body that seemed all curves, clad in a wisp of a dress that showed long, sturdy legs, slits or tears that ran all the way to the top of her thighs, bare arms, and breasts that strained against the fabric. She halted, hands on her hips, the jet black hair hanging loose around a face of high cheekbones, a wide mouth, and lips so full they seemed to be in a constant pout. It was a face and figure that throbbed, and the smile she gave Fargo exuded raw sensuality. She seemed indeed to be a mountain girl—a wild, untamed, pulsating creature. Her eyes stayed on Fargo as she spoke to Linda.

"You didn't say he was so handsome," the girl murmured.

"This is Joey Seaford," Linda introduced. "Tell Fargo about the wagon tracks, Joey," she said.

"What about them?" the girl said, her eyes still on Fargo.

"Did you find them?" he asked her.

"Yep. I knew Linda was looking for tracks. I brought her to see them right after the storm," Joey said, her voice casual, matter-of-fact. "Why, you look for wagon tracks, too?"

"Yes, I am," Fargo said. "Those weren't the right tracks."

The girl's thin black eyebrows lifted, and she gave a half shrug that made her breasts bounce. Her eyes stayed on him, and the sensuality of her was almost palpable, and with it, the very real beauty, tanned and pulsating. She seemed both totally out of place, yet very much in place in this backwoods mountain enclave. Not unlike a Turk's-cap lily in a swamp.

"Stay for noontime vittels, Fargo man," Joey said.

Fargo thought for a moment, aware that everyone in the hollow waited and watched him, if not a threatening air, certainly a judgmental one. Linda's voice whispered beside him. "It's considered an insult to turn down an invitation from Joey," she said.

He offered the girl a smile. "I'd be obliged."

She returned the smile with her own smugness in it. "You won't be sorry," she said, and hurried away. She glided across the ground on bare feet—legs, hips, rear, waist, breasts, all moving in one supple line. He turned to Linda.

"What's the story with her?" he asked.

"Joey is the queen here. Her pa was head of the

Timbersville Mountain colony. Joey became head when he died."

"She's kind of young to head anything, isn't she?" Fargo commented.

"Not here. They obey her and protect her. She's the queen."

"Sort of like a feudal domain," Fargo said.

"More than you know," Linda said. Fargo saw her eyes harden and stay on him. "Are you satisfied about the tracks?" she asked, taking him off to one side.

He drew a deep breath. The wild, sensuous mountain girl wasn't into duplicity or intrigue. Linda couldn't have enlisted her to lie. She'd found the tracks first, not Linda. He met Linda's accusing stare. "Satisfied enough," he said.

"What's that mean?" she snapped.

"It means you probably didn't know the tracks were a false lead," Fargo said.

"Probably?" she shot back.

"Probably," he said. "You could have known even if you didn't find them on your own."

"That's rotten," she hissed.

"I'm giving you the benefit of the doubt," he said.

"It's still rotten," she snapped. "You owe me. You promised. It's time to pay up. Who killed Kenny?"

"I don't know. That's the truth," he said.

"It had to do with the ships, didn't it?" Linda persisted.

"I don't think it did," he said.

"What then? What did he find out?" she asked.

He considered for a moment. Perhaps telling her some things would lessen her certainty the government was to blame. "I think he found out something else, that a double was going to be brought in for somebody important, John Nicolay, Chief of Staff Evan, anybody. I've decided that's what he was trying to tell us with his last word, *double*."

"I think that's reaching," Linda said disdainfully.

"I don't," he said.

"What's Cornelia's place in this?" she questioned.

"I don't know," he answered, unwilling to say more.

"Liar," she threw back. "You trust her. Why?"

"Other people trust her," Fargo said. "That doesn't make her involved."

"Only she is," Linda said.

"You want to believe that."

Linda snorted derisively. "A few years ago the Jeffers family didn't have two nickels to rub together. They had all this land and all those fancy houses and no cash to pay taxes. They were going under. Then Cornelia got friendly with government people in high places. All of a sudden the Jeffers family had money to pay their help and their taxes. She's being paid, and not just for being beautiful."

"They could have paid her for a lot of things, acting as an official hostess at state affairs," he said.

"Then tell me the government didn't have a hand in Kenny's death?"

"I can't. I don't know those things."

"You mean you won't say. You don't keep promises, either. It's contagious, government fever," she said.

"You're running away with yourself," he growled.

"Go to hell, Fargo. I'll find the truth of it, and I'll set it right. I don't need you. You're not helping me, anyway," Linda said, climbed onto the mare, and sent the horse out of the hollow. Fargo turned away, aware it had gone badly, and knew he could do little about it. Linda was still a question mark. Perhaps less of one, but still a question, still an obsessed, angry young woman. He walked away and saw Zeke Cole and Rebecca watching.

"She's not happy with you," the mountain man said.

"Can't help that," Fargo said as Joey returned with two young men carrying tin plates, both in their early twenties, both thin and shallow-faced, both unattractive despite their youth.

"Find a place," she said to Fargo, then lifted her voice. "Noontime vittels," she called out, and the others began to come forward as the two men began handing out the plates. Fargo settled onto a rock; some chose the ground, others logs, a few bringing straight-backed, heavy wood chairs. Joey watched over the two men as they began to fill the plates with stew from one of the kettles, using a deep, long-handled wooden scoop to do so. A thin man with a scraggly beard sat down beside Fargo, hitching up loose, baggy overalls.

"Zed Crabble," he said, introducing himself. Fargo nodded and watched Joey preside over the meal serving, deciding there was an almost ritualistic quality to the event. Two boys came from the trees, two girls following them. The girls were still buttoning their dresses over small, immature breasts, leaves still clinging to their backs. They were no more than thirteen years old, Fargo guessed. "Doin' what comes natural." Zed Crabble chuckled.

"Doing it kind of early, no?" Fargo said with another glance at the two girls.

"Early? We mountain folk don't see it that way," Zed Grabble said.

"How do you see it?" Fargo queried.

"Old enough to bleed, old enough to breed," Zed said with calm logic.

"I think you're upsetting Fargo," a voice said, and Fargo turned to see Joey there with a plate for him, taunting in her eyes. She was definitely older than the two little girls who had come from the trees, but not all that much more, he guessed. "Fargo's been raised with proper down-country manners. He doesn't know our mountain ways." She sat down beside him and leaned back, letting him see the full swell of tanned breasts, the length of sturdy thighs. Maybe age wasn't so important, he felt himself thinking. When in Rome, do as the Romans do, he recalled. "Saw Linda hightailing it through the oaks. Guess you're not her man," Joey said, interrupting his thoughts.

"She ever say I was?" Fargo frowned.

"No. Just figured so."

"Don't figure so quick," he said between bites of the very tasty stew.

"I'm glad. Makes it easier," the young woman said.

"Makes what easier?" Fargo asked.

"What I'm going to say. What has to happen," Joey said as he finished the meal and one of the women took his plate. Joey rose to her feet, reached out, and pulled him with her. He couldn't help but feel the frank, open sensuousness that was part of her every movement. She walked to the side of the trees with him, smiling as they passed one of the young girls lying back, opening her legs for the boy who quickly swarmed over her. "Things are what they are, and we say so here in the mountains," Joey told him. "We have our ways, and we hold to them."

"So it seems," he said as she halted at the edge of the trees and pulled him just inside the shade of the branches where they were suddenly quite alone, separated from the others in the hollow as though there were a wall.

"Things happen, and that's all that matters to us. A tree falls. We don't think about why. The only thing that matters is that it fell. A child dies. We don't spend time looking for reasons we can't likely find or understand, anyway. It happened. Only that matters. Linda brought you here. Why doesn't matter. I saw you and knew you were the one." She paused, smiling with a sudden maturity beyond her years. "Ever since Pa died, I've waited for someone strong, someone from outside. It was to be. Everyone knew it. I just had to wait, and now it's happened. You are here, for me."

"You saying what I think you are?" he asked, a mixture of emotions coursing through him.

"I'm saying what must be." Joey smiled almost benignly. "You, me, together. You taking me, giving yourself to me. You will like it, believe me, Fargo, staying here, being here with me."

"I don't doubt that. It's sure flattering and sure tempting, but I've a job to do. I can't forget about it."

"Finding the wagon trails?" she asked, a sudden slyness in her voice. He frowned at her and nodded. "I know about a lot of wagon trails," she said.

"You've seen them?" he asked.

"Yes. I can find them again for you. Stay with me and I will."

Thoughts raced through his mind. He had to be careful not to turn her away as he coaxed more from her. "It's not that simple. Finding the trails is only part of it. There's a lot more, such as where they go, what they're doing, carrying."

The sly little smile touched her pouty lips again. "I might know a lot more," she said.

"Do you?" he tossed at her sharply.

"Will you?" she shot back.

He smiled. Joey knew how to parry. Bargaining was part of the mountain ways, plainly. His answer tossed inside him. She was all throbbing sensuality. Making love to her would be eminently exciting. Being a mountain man stud was less so. Yet she had given him a choice he couldn't turn down, one that guaranteed pleasure as it promised success. He'd really nothing to lose and everything to gain. When it was over, when he'd finished with the wagons and was surfeited with Joey, he'd find a way to disentangle himself. Even pleasure had its limits. But for now she offered answers he needed and enjoyment he'd welcome. He reached up and pressed the back of his hand against her young, smooth face.

"Can't turn away from what has to be," he said.

A slightly smug smile touched her lips. "Can't hold back what I know," she murmured, bringing her full lips up to press his, lips terribly soft and enveloping, made for giving every kind of pleasure. But he finally pulled back. He'd already decided he had to have Cornelia in on the answers. He wanted her to see for herself before she put countermoves into motion again.

"I want someone else to see the trails and everything else you can show me" he said. "My boss. It's important. I'll be back by morning. I answer to others." She thought, pouted for a moment, then nodded.

"Hurry," she said, and waved to him as he took the Ovaro, tossed a wave at the others in the hollow, and retraced his way down the narrow passage. He stopped at the cabin as the day drew to a close, slept a few hours, and was riding before dawn. He reached Washington and Cornelia's town mansion by midmorning, and she met him, wearing a deep yellow shirt and black riding britches, flame red hair freshly brushed and glinting of fire.

"We hit the mother lode," he told her. "Get your horse. We'll talk on the way." She hurried away and minutes later rode beside him from the capital. He told her about Joey and the mountain colony, unable to contain his excitement. Cornelia listened, her face beautifully quiet.

"She hasn't shown you anything yet," Cornelia said.

"I stopped her. I wanted you to be there," Fargo said. "But she knows, not just the wagon tracks, but where they go and a lot more. She can give us everything we want. I'm sure of it. She knows the mountains. They're her home." Cornelia nodded, but her face remained still. "Figured you'd be more excited," Fargo remarked.

"I will be when we're sure. That last fiasco is still with me," Cornelia said as she reached out and closed a hand on his arm. "The only thing good to come of it is that you're still alive."

"This'll be different," he said, and set a steady pace that finally brought them to the narrow, winding passage dense with oak. When he emerged into the hollow, Cornelia quickly brought her horse up beside him. Fargo scanned the hollow, the ramshackle huts, the three steaming kettles at the rear, and halted, dismounted, and gave Cornelia a hand down from the buckskin. The mountain men and their women began to come forward, staring at Cornelia, and he saw Zeke Cole with his mouth hanging open as he took her in. Sarah and Hedda Cole came with him, also staring at Cornelia. The others also approached, some frowning, some simply staring. A little girl reached up and touched Cornelia's full, flowing tresses of fiery red.

Fargo heard the sound of the leaves being brushed back and turned as Joey swung to the ground on her rope. Her black eyes bored into Cornelia, her throbbing sensuality transformed into wild fury. Her eyes went to Fargo, fury blazing in the black orbs. "What is this? What in damn hell's fire are you doing?" she screamed.

"Easy, now, Joey. This is my boss, Cornelia Jeffers," Fargo said.

Joey shot a look of disdain at him. "That's a damn lie. You've brought your woman with you."

"No, she's my boss," he said, trying to avoid unwieldy explanations.

"No woman's your boss. You're lying, and you lied to me," Joey said, her body shaking, and he saw one of the top buttons of the already abbreviated dress pop open. "You'd no right, no right at all, after what you promised. Bringing her here is not our ways."

"I wanted Cornelia to see what you were going to show me," Fargo said placatingly. "It's important she knows, too."

"Show you? Show you?" Joey flung back. "I'll not be showing you anything now. Take her and get out of here."

"Joey, listen to me," he tried, but Joey backed away.

"Go, goddammit, go. Take her and go. Now, now, now," Joey screamed.

He felt Cornelia pull on him as she climbed onto the buckskin. "Come on, dammit," she said.

Joey started to almost run toward the rear of the hollow. "Joey, wait," he called, but she kept on. "I'll come back. We'll talk about this," he said.

"No. Never. Not with her," Joey shouted, a mixed message, fury the only certain thing in it. Fargo swept the others with a long glance, saw their faces were rigid, disapproving, hostile. Zeke Cole spoke up for the rest.

"Joey promised herself to you. You agreed, and you come here with another woman. You insulted Joey, insulted all of us. Get out of here while you can," he said.

Fargo swung himself onto the Ovaro, afraid anything he'd say or do could only escalate the ugly confrontation. Joey knew too much to let a misunderstanding destroy everything. He'd not understood their damn backwoods mountain codes. He'd have to make his apologies. But this wasn't the moment. There was too much anger, too much stiff-backed outrage. Cornelia was already at the opening of the passage, and he caught up to her and led the way down the twisting, narrow path. He didn't say anything until they finally emerged from the passage and rode onto a flat ridge. "Guess bringing you was a big mistake," he muttered.

"Maybe," Cornelia said.

"Didn't see much maybe to it," he grunted.

"Maybe," she repeated, and he shot her a quizzical glance.

"You want to explain that?" he asked.

"Later. Come back to Washington with me," she said.

"I was figuring on going back to Joey, mend fences."

"We'll talk about that later, too," Cornelia said. He shrugged consent. Perhaps it was best not to go back to Joey right away, he reflected. It might be wiser to give her time to cool off. His decision made, he set a fast pace. Cornelia rode with her face much more relaxed than it had been on the way to the mountains, he noticed, and the day was over when they finally reached the mansion. She had servants scramble up something to eat and drink, and finally he finished the meal with a good rich port. Cornelia led him into a small study as the house grew dark and silent. "I know you want to go back looking for wagon tracks," she said.

"Have to. I can't expect you or Stanton to commit another force without solid information this time," he said.

"That's right. I wouldn't ask it. But going back to her and the mountain people isn't the answer." Cornelia smiled and took one of his hands in hers. "You still don't understand what happened up there. You didn't make a mistake in bringing me, not really. That was a good excuse for her." Fargo frowned, and Cornelia's smile widened. "She doesn't know anything. She had no wagon tracks to give you, no anything else. That was all a wonderfully clever way to get what she wanted, you."

"Can't see that. She knew I'd want to see tracks," Fargo said.

"And she'd have a hundred ways to fool you, put you off. I watched her. She has a lot of ways built in that no man could refuse. Even if there were tracks, they were probably old and meaningless. She's smart as well as a wild little thing. But when she saw me, she knew she'd have to produce. The game was up. She knew it at once and gave a wonderful performance. It was a very good act, but that's what it was."

"The others went along. They have some kind of code," he said.

"I'm sure they do, and little Joey knew the right time to use it," Cornelia said. "She had nothing to give you, believe me. I saw through her right away. That throbbing sensuality didn't have any effect on me. She'd like you to go back so she could have another shot at you. I'm sure that sensuality is part of what's pulling you back there. She offered you a lot more than wagon tracks." He didn't answer, but couldn't help a wry smile. Cornelia touched a truth— Perhaps astuteness, sharpness, or just her womanly wisdom. "There's no need for you to go back to her," Cornelia said. "I'll prove it to you."

She leaned forward, her mouth coming on his, smooth moistness, still at first, then working, small nibbling motions, and he felt the very tip of her tongue come out and draw in at once. But her hand came over his, pressing his palm against one warm, deep breast, and he heard her tiny gasp. He held her gently, and she rose and pulled him with her into an adjoining room where he saw the big double bed, light blue satin on it that matched the blue of the bedroom walls. She halted alongside the bed and slowly began to unbutton the yellow shirt, letting it hang open, and he glimpsed the sides of her breasts. Her fingers touched the jodhpurs, and they fell away as she stepped from them, flung off pantaloons, and then the blouse, and stood beautifully naked before him. But not just naked. She was a magnificent, living, painting come to life—statuesque beauty with every part of her shimmering. The flame red hair hung loose around her shoulders and below it. Two breasts thrust forward with a kind of defiance, full and round and deep and beautifully erect. A large, deep red circle tipped each and surrounded surprisingly small red nipples.

A deep rib cage fit the sturdy, well-formed hips, and he took in legs that were strong yet curvey, thighs sturdy yet sleek. A rounded belly tapered into a strong V adorned with a very full, very black nap that perfectly matched the rest of her. She waited, letting him enjoy her statuesque beauty before she came to him and pulled at his clothes. He helped her shed his garments and tossed gun belt and calf holster on the floor as she lay back on the bed. He took another moment to drink in the sheer beauty of her, from flame red hair to long, sturdy calves.

She smiled as she enjoyed the appreciation in his eyes, and when he came to her, he saw the thin veil move across the agate green eyes and her lips parted for him. She pressed her mouth to his, worked her lips, then let her tongue dart out and circle his, messages sent, silent whispers given. She turned, pulled back, and lifted one full, deep breast to him, and he curled his lips around its warm fullness. "Yes, oh yes," Cornelia murmured, a throaty sound, as his tongue slowly circled the little nipple, then pulled gently on the thin little filaments that lay around the edges of the areola. He played with each deep breast and little tip, and Cornelia moved her body back and forth, up, then down, her magnificent figure seeming to dance horizontally. His hand slid downward across the deep rib cage onto the roundness of her belly, paused to touch the oblong indentation, then moved down again.

He found the dense, bushy, black nap and pushed through it, letting his fingers tangle in the fibrous brush. He felt the warm rise under it and pressed down upon the Venus mound. Cornelia cried out in delight. "Oh, yes, ah, aaaaah," she moaned, and his hand moved farther down. When he pushed into the warm softness between her thighs, her moans became guttural cries. Her legs fell open, and her hips rose, swung around, and her hand came up, closed around his throbbing fullness, and she stroked, pulled, caressed. "Yes, yes, let me, give me," she cried, then brought her torso up and rubbed the black bushy V over him, reveling in touch, sensation, the pleasure of the tactile.

Suddenly, almost abruptly, she swung her legs up and over, straddled his hips, and slowly, with surprising delicateness, she slid over him. "Aaaaaah, ah,

Jesus . . . oh, yes, yes," she moaned, and he felt the sweet wetness of her encompassing him—ultimate, eternal embrace, ecstasy forever new yet forever the same. Cornelia enveloped him, sliding her tunneled softness up and down him, her deep breasts brought up to his face. Her magnificent body surged forward, drew back, and surged again, each movement deliciously overwhelming. He took her torso, turned, and rolled her onto her back. Cornelia's cry was a guttural hymn to pleasure as he thrust deeper into her. Her legs lifted, came up and embraced his hips, then held him as she grasped hold of ecstasy. Her hair fell wildly, a fiery shower, and the deep, full breasts quivered under his lips. He heard the change in her deep moans, a sudden urgency coming into them, and knew what it signaled. Her thighs tightened around him as her hips thrust upward. "Harder, harder," she screamed, and in seconds she tossed and lifted, a woman possessed by ecstasy, magnificent beauty made more so by the torrent of pleasure that engulfed him as well.

He was with her when she came, every part of her stiffening for a fleeting instant, then twisting, writhing, surging against him, deep, full breasts pushing upward and the flame red hair falling around him as he caressed her breasts. "Yes . . . ah, yeeeees," Cornelia cried out as her groin pushed into his and her cries spiraled through the room, finally breaking off in a half cry, half moan of ecstasy and despair. She clung hard for another minute, then fell back onto the bed, gasping, and he watched her breasts rise and fall, her full legs slide against each other, and finally lie still. On one elbow he looked at her and marveled again at her sheer beauty, breathtaking even in repose.

She turned, sighed, came against him, and he found one deep breast against his face. He fell asleep holding her and woke when morning came. She sat up and let a wise little smile touch her lips as he enjoyed the way her breasts gently swayed. "You see you don't need any little mountain girl," Cornelia said.

"Guess not," he said.

"Forget her and the mountains and wagon tracks. I've never believed the ships come that way. They're being brought in somewhere along the upper Chesapeake, maybe down the Susquehanna from Pennsylvania," Cornelia said as she swung from the bed and took a light robe from a chair. "I have to meet with John Nicolay, maybe the president. I might be a day, maybe two. Stay here if you want," she said, then allowed a wry smile. "But you won't, of course," she said.

"Can't find any wagon tracks in bed," he said.

"And not in those damn mountains, either. Remember what I said, somewhere along the Susquehanna," Cornelia said, then leaned over and pressed her breasts into his face. "And remember last night. Whenever you want," she said and stood up. The agate green eyes enjoyed him as she let him take in all the flame haired, voluptuous beauty of her for another moment before she pulled the robe around herself. She hurried away, and he lay back, listening to her dressing and finally the door closing as she left.

Thoughts instantly crowded each other. Surprisingly, he found they were of mountain hollows and a young, wild mountain girl. Cornelia had dismissed Joey completely. Perhaps it was easy for her. It wasn't for him. It wasn't the lure of wild, throbbing sexuality. Cornelia had supplied enough of that. With purpose, she'd taken lust out of the equation. He smiled. But not anything else. He couldn't accept Cornelia's explanation of Joey's rage or the strange codes of backwoods mountain folk. A performance, Cornelia had called Joey's explosion, empty as anything else she'd promised, a wonderful act. But Cornelia had reacted understandably to an ominous scene. She hadn't seen Joey but for a few brief moments. That throbbing sensuality was no performance. That couldn't be faked.

It no doubt helped her get her way, was part of her very being, and it was real. Joey was what she was, spoiled, arrogant, demanding, but there was no trickery to her, no fakery. He'd bet on that. He hadn't suddenly forgotten how to read signs. Joey was real, that was one certainty. Acting wasn't part of her. She hadn't lied about wagon tracks or other things. He wanted another chance to prove that, he muttered as he swung from the bed. He owed that to himself, and perhaps to Joey. Perhaps even to Linda, he reflected, though she was off on her own and out of his way. He was glad for that. He washed quickly, dressed, and found a quill pen and an inkstand on a desk and left Cornelia a note.

"Have to give the mountains another try. Be back when I've something to report. Fargo," he wrote and left the note on the bed. The Ovaro was brought around, and he had just pulled himself into the saddle when the dark blue navy carriage drove up and Captain Winslow stepped from it.

"Fargo, glad to see you. I've come to see Cornelia," the captain said.

"She's not here," Fargo said.

Winslow's lips tightened. "We're hearing all kinds of rumors, another shipment of those damn cutters coming through, secessionist moves being strengthened. It's not looking good. I want to hear what Cornelia can tell me," he said.

"I understand she's meeting with John Nicolay," Fargo said.

"Meetings that aren't doing anything," Winslow exploded. "Another shipment of those cutters could tip the balance against us. They know our movements, where our ships are, but we can't get a line on them. You haven't come up with anything, either, Fargo."

"Not yet," Fargo agreed grimly.

"It's plain that their intelligence is better than ours. I'm worried, Fargo, real worried," Winslow said. "We were counting on you for a breakthrough."

"Don't stop, not yet," Fargo said.

"I'll hang in. Don't have any other choice," the captain said, and retired into the carriage. Fargo put the Ovaro into a canter as he rode west out of the capital and toward the mountains.

11

There was little more than an hour left to the day when the big black-and-white horse nosed its way into the deep hollow. Fargo slowly scanned the scene, taking in the ramshackle huts, the cleared area, and the three huge iron kettles at the rear, bubbling and steaming. He saw the figures stare at him in shock, then start toward him, men and women, the men taking their long-barreled varmint rifles. He focused on Zeke Cole as the man approached him, Rebecca, Hedda, and Sarah coming with him. Other bearded men came, everyone frowning at him.

"You must be out of your skull, mister, comin' here like you was welcome," Zeke Cole said.

"Insultin' us again, you are," one of the Crabbles chimed in. "Insultin' Joey, too." Others came forward, anger in each face, rifles being raised. Fargo swung down from the Ovaro, surprising them, and they halted. He had already made a decision on how he'd handle it—take them off guard, no showing fear, not even respect.

"Cowshit," he bit out. "Didn't insult her before. Not insulting her now. Same with you. Where is she?"

Zeke Cole raised his voice, yelling into the nearby trees, "Abel, get out here." Fargo's eyes went to the trees, held there until the branches moved and the figure appeared. A man wearing trousers and tattered suspenders over a torn undershirt came toward him, resembling a house with legs, a huge form over six feet and probably close to three hundred pounds. A jowly, heavy face almost enfolded small slit eyes. Broad cheekbones and thick lips completed the impression of borderline intelligence. "He's come back, Abel," Zeke Cole said, and the man focused his slit eyes on Fargo as he lumbered forward. Fargo saw the man's bull-like shoulders, a chest that was all power, and arms that resembled small tree trunks.

"You made yourself a real big mistake, mister," the huge figure rumbled. "Now I have to smash you into little pieces."

"Who the hell are you?" Fargo tossed back.

"Abel is Joey's bodyguard. He's been made her protector," Zeke Cole said. "Her pa picked him for it."

"You shouldn't have insulted Joey," Abel said. Fargo's hand went to the Colt.

"I wouldn't do that," one of the Crabbles said, and Fargo saw at least six varmint rifles pointed at him. "We don't take to gunfighting here," the man said. "This is going to be a fair fight, one on one. Now let's have that pistol." Fargo hesitated. He was more than fast enough to take most of them. But most wasn't all.

180

Besides, he didn't want a shoot-out that would bring only killing and no answers. But they weren't anxious for that, either, he was sure. The Colt was still a bargaining chip.

"You play with your mountain codes. I came to see Joey," Fargo said. "Get her, or it'll be a helluva shoot-out."

"Speak your piece," a voice said, and he saw Joey step from behind one of the shacks, clothed in the same torn, tight, form-fitting garment. She exuded the same throbbing sensuality, only now a combination of anger and hurt added a new, darker layer.

"You had it all wrong," he said.

She shrugged. "Words come easy. You didn't do right," she said. "Besides, it's past fixing now."

"But not past fighting," he grunted.

"I won't turn away those who look after me," she said. "I've no right." She was telling him something obliquely, as best she could. She couldn't go against the mountain code, even if she was tempted. They needed her, and she needed them. He grimaced inwardly as he made his decision. The best of a bad bargain, perhaps, but he had to take it. He turned to the huge man, then to the others.

"I want it to mean something," he said, taking Joey in with his glance. "I win, and you show me the tracks and everything else you know. I win, and there's no holding back anything. Abel wins, and I'm yours, for whatever, whenever."

Joey's black eyes bored into him, then turned to Abel. "Win for me, Abel," she said.

The little slit eyes somehow managed to glint. "He's yours, if I don't happen to kill him," Abel rumbled.

"Don't do that. Just win," Joey told the hulk.

"Your pistol, mister," Zeke Cole said, and Fargo lifted the Colt and tossed it on the ground. They pushed a little boy forward to pick it up and bring it to them. Fargo shot Joey a glance, and she looked away as she stepped to one side of the hollow. Abel began to move toward him, Fargo saw, long arms swinging easily. The man carried a layer of fat, but beneath it there was a mountain of muscle, Fargo was certain. He could take no chances with the hulking figure, and he began to circle as the others stepped back to leave plenty of room at the center of the hollow. Bearded men, their womenfolk, half-naked children, young boys and girls, all of them looking on, an intently silent audience. Another quick glance showed him Joey, alone, off to one side, her face impassive.

Abel moved in, a sudden lunge forward as he swung a long-armed left hook, a wild blow Fargo easily ducked away from. Abel lunged again, this time a right hook, and again Fargo easily ducked the blow. Abel plodded forward, his huge bulk managing to weave, not unlike a big oak bending in the wind. He feinted with a left, threw a right, but this time Fargo slipped the blows and sent his own straight, jolting jab out and had the pleasure of seeing Abel's head snap back. Fargo stepped in, shot another stiff jab, then another. The man roared as he lunged, swinging roundhouse blows with both hands. Fargo parried each, danced aside, and countered with another two hard jabs, then a short left hook. He'd box the hulk, he decided, wear him down first. He shot out another two jabs, but Abel plowed forward as though the blows hadn't landed.

Fargo feinted, shot out a whistling left, then a follow-up right. The hulking figure stopped in his tracks, blinked, and came forward again. Fargo repeated the maneuver, feinted, then followed with two powerhouse blows to Abel's jaw. Again the huge figure stopped, blinked, and came forward. Fargo threw the next blows without feinting, connecting with six punches, any one of which would have put the ordinary man down. Blood ran from Abel's thick lips, but his broad face showed no change of expression, and Fargo felt the pain in his arms from the punches. Suddenly, Abel lunged forward, not swinging wild blows this time, and Fargo brought up a short, hard uppercut. It landed on Abel's jaw, and the mountainous figure's head snapped back. But only for an instant, and he dived forward again. He raised a huge arm and deflected Fargo's left cross, then brought his own right up in a wide arc. Fargo brought an arm up to parry the blow, but felt his defense swept away and pain shoot through his arm as Abel's blow smashed into it.

Ducking, Fargo dropped low to bring up a straight left and right, but the huge bulk was on him, and he felt his blows brushed aside. Abel's treelike arms closed around him, his weight bending him backward. Fargo felt himself going down, then he twisted and brought up a knee that caught his huge foe in the belly. Abel let out a grunt and dropped to one knee. Fargo twisted away from the giant's grip. The tremendous blow, delivered hammerlike, smashed into Fargo's back. Fargo felt pain shoot through his entire body, but he managed to kick, pull free, and, his back afire, he turned and regained his feet as Abel charged again. Fargo threw a straight left and a right, the pain shooting through his arms as the blows landed, but Abel kept coming, his chin now coated with blood.

Twisting away, grimacing as his back sent waves of pain through him, he avoided Abel's lunge, then spun as the man turned to lunge again. Stepping in, Fargo sunk a pile-driver blow into his opponent's midsection. Abel grunted, let out a gasp of air, and dropped to one knee. Fargo leaped in with a hard left that caught his foe high on the cheekbone and sent a shower of red into the air. Abel roared, drove his huge bulk upward, brushed aside Fargo's two quick blows as though they were annoyances, and reached for his opponent with treelike arms outstretched. Fargo saw the powerful arms close around his neck, but brought both his own arms upward in a kind of double uppercut. Abel staggered for a moment, his grip loosened, and Fargo pulled away, delivering another blow to Abel's face. Again Abel merely shook his head and came forward, head lowered, a charging bull. Suddenly, his arms tired from smashing blows at the hulk, Fargo realized that not only was Abel a mountain of paper, he was hardly aware of pain.

Those with borderline intelligence often had no sensitivity to pain, he had heard. Abel was proving it.

But with no choice, Fargo lashed out again, a quick rain of blows. Abel's broad face was dripping with blood now, but the slit eyes still peered out. He came forward, and Fargo drew back, dancing away despite the searing pain in his back. He ducked low, then came up with a roundhouse left that sent Abel onto his heels. Seeing an opportunity, Fargo threw a right cross, then another left. Abel staggered back again, and Fargo grew careless, following too quickly with another left. Abel got an arm up, blocked the blow, and backhanded, smashing his tremendous arm into Fargo's face. Fargo felt himself go backward and down, his head exploding with colored lights. He half turned, a reflex action, and shook his head to clear it as he felt himself being lifted up into the air as though he were a child.

His head cleared as he sailed across the center of the hollow, hit the ground, and again desperately shook his head as searing pain engulfed him. He managed to turn in time to see Abel bringing a ham-like fist down, a sideways blow. Turning, Fargo took the blow on his upper forearm as his entire body shook. He twisted on the ground and tried to roll away, but this time never saw the kick that smashed into him. But he felt it as breath seemed to rush from his chest and his ribs cried out. Trying to draw in breath, he twisted again, somehow avoided another hammerlike blow, and scooted forward. Abel followed, but even racked with pain as he was, Fargo was still quicker. He avoided the hulk's wild blows, rolled again and came up on one knee, then pushed to his feet.

He could barely breathe, and every part of his body seemed afire. He tried another left as the hulk came at him, then realized he hadn't any snap in his blows now. Abel's bloodied face seemed a mask from hell, only the slit eyes still visible, and yet he came forward. Fargo gave ground, unwilling to waste punches that didn't have power. He danced backward as the hulk, sensing he had the upper hand, lumbered forward, treelike arms raised, ready to punch or parry. Fargo, aware he had little strength left in his pain-racked body, knew he had to conserve what he still had for one last attack. He moved backward, and side to side, his eyes flicking to the edges of the hollow, where he scanned the silent audience. He didn't see Joey, but he did glimpse something else, and he began to move in a zigzag line.

Abel plodded after him with more speed than he'd shown before. Fargo flicked out blows, jabs and more jabs, blows aimed at irritating Abel, keeping him plowing forward. Casting another quick glance behind him, Fargo saw he was almost at one of the big iron kettles that steamed and bubbled. He shot out another jab, then one more as he gave further ground. The hulking form bored in, now certain victory was near, his foe on the run. With a further quick glance behind, Fargo saw the moment was at hand. He threw another jab, harder this time, but Abel ignored it and swung his own wild blow. Fargo braced himself, took the blow on his forearm, and let himself fall to one knee. Abel roared, a blood-spattering, primitive sound, and charged. Fargo stayed low and counted off the last split second as Abel reached him, then he dived down. He hit the huge form at the ankles, and, screaming with the pain that shot through his body, he rose, summoning up a last reserve of strength.

He lifted the hulking figure, letting his strength and Abel's momentum combine, then saw the man sail over his head and go facedown into the huge kettle. A muffled scream of agony rose up from the kettle, the man's torso and legs shaking wildly, thrashing the air. Fargo rose, stepped back, and saw Zeke Cole and others starting to run toward the kettle. They reached Abel's legs, a half dozen of them pulling him from the kettle. But Abel's wild thrashing had stopped, as had his muffled screams. They pulled him out and laid him on the ground, where little trails of steam rose into the air from his scorched and seared body.

They stared down at the still, mountainous form and slowly lifted their eyes to Fargo, who had pushed to his feet, managing to stand despite the pain that consumed his every muscle. "I'd use one of the other kettles for dinner," Fargo said. They stared at him with awe and grudging admiration, he saw.

"By God, mister. I'd never have believed it," Zeke Cole muttered. Fargo drew in breath very carefully, each one filled with pain. He saw the black-haired figure come toward him, halt, and search his face.

"Can you walk?" Joey asked.

"Real slow," he said.

She put an arm around his waist and led him into the trees, through thick foliage to where a house suddenly appeared. Less ramshackle than the others, it had a solid roof and glass in the windows. He followed her into a living room with a tattered sofa, two chairs, and a hearth. She took him into an adjoining room with a big bed, a low, ancient dresser, and a hooked rug on the floor that added almost elegance.

"Lie down," she said, and he groaned in pain as he stretched out on the bed. He watched as she began to undress him, gently and slowly, her eyes taking in the muscled beauty of his body, lingering at one place, and finally moving on. "Turn over," she said, went to the dresser, and brought back a staghorn bottle. Sitting on the bed beside him, she began to apply a cool ointment to his shoulders and back.

"Feels good," he said.

"Hyssop, white willow bark compress, lobelia, and comfrey. Been a mountain recipe for generations." She massaged the salve all over his body, and he was almost asleep when she finished, dimly aware that night had fallen. "Sleep," she said, and he was happy to oblige.

When he woke, he heard the songbirds, and the little room was filled with sunlight. He swung long legs over the edge of the bed, surprised at how little pain he felt. He stepped to the doorway, saw the other room was empty, and went to the front door. He heard the stream behind the trees, followed the sound of it, and let the cool water wash the salve from him.

He returned to the house, sat naked in a square of sun until he dried off, and then pulled on clothes. He'd just finished when Joey appeared carrying a basket of wild cherries and a half dozen biscuits. She wore another dress, identical to the first one, except it was blue, the tears and cuts in it at almost the exact same spots. She set the basket down and sat beside him as he ate, joining in with the biscuits. "That ointment did real well," he said. She nodded, unsmiling.

"You sorry I won?" he slid at her.

She took a moment before answering. "Glad for you, sorry for me," she said finally. She put one tanned, beautifully smooth, sturdy leg up on the back of a chair.

"I'm not changing anything," he said.

"Would not ask you."

He allowed a wry smile. "Good. Now let's go riding," he said and walked with her as she led the way through the dense foliage and into the hollow. One of the Crabbles came toward him with the Colt.

"This here's yours," the man said. Fargo took the gun, holstered it, and saw the others watching him with new respect. Joey brought a short-legged, dark gray mixed-blood out of the trees and swung onto it, using only a blanket saddle, Indian fashion. He followed her as she rode from the hollow west along a hickory-lined forest, then upward until she reached a tree-covered ledge. She turned south, and he rode beside her as the ledge widened, stayed tree-covered, but with wide lanes that paralleled each other. Joey turned west, followed one of the lanes as it widened farther, and reined up, pointing to the ground.

Fargo rode past her and frowned as he saw the wheel tracks appear from another lane. He pulled to a halt, dismounted, and began to walk alongside the tracks. Squatting down, he ran his fingers across the wagon tracks and looked across at the imprint of hoofmarks alongside the wagon marks. He was still frowning as Joey came beside him, and he glanced up at her. "These the only ones?" he asked.

"Yes." She nodded. "Why?"

He grimaced. "It's not right."

"There are no others. They have been moving this way for months. I see new tracks every time I come up here. They move only at night," Joey said.

"That figures," Fargo muttered, his eyes going to the hoofprints. "Riders going along with them. That's in order." He walked slowly alongside the wheel marks, studying each. They tended to run into one another, overlapping, but he brought all his knowledge to bear, studied the width of each track, and saw where the marks pushed against each other. "Eight wagons, at least, maybe ten or twelve. That figures, too." He pinched the edges of one track between his thumb and forefinger. "These aren't more than a day or two old," he said, and peered down the tree-covered lane until the wagon tracks faded from his vision. "They're going in the right direction," he said, talking to himself more than to Joey.

"Then what's wrong?" she asked.

"These tracks were made by wagons too small to

carry what I want. These are tracks from mountain wagons, maybe even farm wagons. Too small, all of them," Fargo said.

"Then why do they sneak through the mountains, move only by night?"

He pondered the question for a long moment. "I don't know. They could be smuggling something else, nothing to do with what I have to find," he said.

She shrugged, swung onto the short-legged horse, and started back to the hollow. Fargo followed her as, nearing the hollow, she turned and pushed through the thick foliage to the house. She dismounted, a lithe, graceful motion as dusk began to slide over the mountains. He swung to the ground and followed her into the house. "I showed you the tracks," Joey said. "I've kept my part of it."

"You said you knew more," he reminded her.

"I know where the tracks go," Joey said. "I followed them a good ways."

"Where?"

"Down to the caves just above Deer Wallow. It's the only place they could have gone," Joey said.

"Caves?" Fargo frowned.

"That part of the Shenandoah is made of big caves, at least six of them, good for storing anything. In winter we use one to store dried beef," Joey said.

Fargo frowned into space, his thoughts returning to what he'd told her about the tracks. His explanation grew more plausible the more he thought about it.

"They're still not the tracks I'm after," he said. "I'm not going on another wild-goose chase. The last one was a decoy, a trap set up and closed on me. But if somebody else is doing their own thing through the mountains, they can do it. I've no time to waste on curiosity."

"You going back come morning?" she asked.

"Figure to, or keep on looking somewhere else," he said.

She faced him, hands on her hips, her full lips forming a pout as her black eyes smoldered. "You won. You set the rules. I abided by them," she said. "But you do not have to. You can stay."

"And you'd have what you want with no right to it," he said.

She glowered back. "I was wrong about the woman," she said. "That doesn't change what should be, for me, for all of us here in the Timbersville. It doesn't change that."

"I don't fancy being used as a stud," he said.

"You think that's all it is?"

"You make it sound that way."

"It's only a part. Most everything is me. I can prove that real quick," she said. He didn't answer, and her hand came to the top of the torn dress, flipped open buttons, and in what seemed but seconds she was standing naked before him, proud defiance adding to her throbbing sensuality. She hadn't Cornelia's breathtaking statuesqueness, but she very much had her own beauty, a body sturdy and pulsating, her breasts full and well formed, each with a deep red tip and matching areola. He took in wide hips, a rounded belly, and just below it, a profuse, black V. Deeply

192

tanned legs presented well-curved thighs, all of her compact and brimming with throbbing sensuousness.

She backed slowly into the bedroom, her eyes holding him, and he followed, realizing he was almost hypnotized by the pulsating vibrations she exuded. He pulled off clothes as she lay back on the bed, and she half rose as he came to her, eyes wide, focused on his throbbing maleness. Her arms came around him, an almost desperate clutch, and he felt her hands slide down his body and close around him. "Good, oh, good, good, good," Joey breathed and pushed her breasts upward. He closed his mouth around one full breast, pulled, and felt the deep red tip instantly stiffen. He caressed the quivering nipple, then brought his mouth up to hers, and Joey answered with her lips enveloping his, her tongue darting out— wild, eager messages. He brought his mouth back to her breast. "Yes, yes, yes . . . oh, more, more," she cried out, her voice deep, her full thighs sliding up and down against his hips, her body thrusting upward, consumed with her own eagerness.

His hand moved down across the convex mound of her belly, caressed the smooth roundness of it, and pushed through the tangled nap just below. Joey's half scream was an almost animal cry. Her hand came up, clapped over his, pressed his palm down on her pubic mound, and held it there as her hips rose, swiveled, then fell back. Her sturdy thighs came open, and her skin felt suddenly damp. She pushed against his hand again, bringing it down to the dark portal that yawned for him. "Come, come, come, oh come to me, Fargo, come to me," Joey gasped, and he felt all the throbbing sexuality of her exploding. Her black hair flew from side to side as her head turned and twisted and her mouth worked feverishly, pulling in air, mumbling, half crying until he pressed his lips to her. "Mmmmm . . . mmmmm . . . good, good," she cried, and her hand had hold of him, pushing him into her. "Come, come, oh, God, come," she murmured, and he thrust forward, surprised at her tightness, heard her tiny cry, and then her scream of pleasure.

She rose with him, fell with him, pushed and pulled and twisted, her breasts rolling from one side to the other and back again as she seemed utterly consumed with her own wildness. He felt himself carried along with her and thrust deeply, then stayed, pulled back, and thrust again, falling in with her rhythm. "Oh, good, oh, good, oh good," Joey cried out with each driving shaft, almost singing out the words, and she pulled his face down to one vibrating nipple, held it there. Even before he heard her rising cry, he felt her gathering, every honeyed sensation coming together for that culminating moment of ecstasy. He was ready, going with her as her hips rose and she quivered against him, little wild cries falling from her lips. She pressed tight against him, every part of her pulsating body aquiver, and suddenly her sturdy legs tightened hard against him. "Oh, God, now, now, now, now," she screamed, and he exploded with her, spiraled with her, reached the peak of peaks with her, and held her there until finally, with a half cry she fell back.

He continued to stay with her and felt the pulsing of her as she lay with him, her tiny cries pressing into his chest. She half turned, brought one full breast to him, and held it there until she finally lay still, arms and legs falling open with a kind of sweet surrender. She brought herself together after a while and pushed onto one elbow, her smile holding all the wisdom of the world in it. "I was right, from that very first time," she said. "I knew you would be like this, right for me, everything I could want."

"Good," he said as she came against him, settling down, and he heard her fall asleep quickly. The small candle burning in a corner of the room afforded just enough flickering light to see her sturdy beauty. He hadn't noticed the candle in the day. She plainly kept it burning constantly. The thick foliage rustled against the roof of the house, and he fell asleep with her, staying asleep until just before dawn when he woke as he felt tingling pleasure going through him, translated sensations that became lips, tongue, mouth, caressing, pulling, drawing in. He reached for her, and she came up, pressing her tanned smooth skin tight to him, and turned the last of the night into new fire. Sunlight slid into the room when she lay with him, eyes closed, half asleep, surfeited and satisfied. When he woke again, the sun filling the room, she sat up, a smug smile touching her face, pulled him to his feet, and went to the brook with him, naked as inhabitants in the Garden of Eden.

Once again she found wild cherries to breakfast on, and he dressed when they finished. "You're full of surprises," he told her.

"You said you were going to leave today. I didn't want only one time," she said with honesty, leaning forward and pressing her breasts against him.

"You're persistent, too." He laughed, and she smiled as she shrugged. He went from the house with her, then halted as a line of bearded mountain men trudged through the woods, each carrying a one-man handsaw. He recognized Elwood Crabble in the lead. "Firewood?" he asked her.

"No," she said, took his hand, and led him after the eight figures. When the thick trees thinned some, he saw the eight figures beside a big black oak that had fallen. It lay stretched along the ground, at least thirty feet of it. Some of the eight men were sawing at the base of the tree, others were sawing into the trunk higher up, and still others were trimming off branches. He stepped closer with Joey and received a nod from Elwood Crabble. "We want to put the tree along one side of the hollow so it'll break up the rainwater that comes down and floods us," Joey said. "We want the whole tree, but we could never move it in one piece."

"Too big and heavy," Elwood Crabble put in. "So we're cutting it into pieces we can move. When we get it in place, we'll put it back together again."

"You could use the right kind of tools. Those handsaws will take forever. You need double-handled bucking saws, crosscut saws, broadaxes, and falling axes with double-bit heads," Fargo said.

"We make do with what we have," Elwood Crabble said and returned to his sawing. Joey turned and started to walk away. Fargo went with her, his thoughts still on Elwood Crabble and the others. He found himself feeling sorry for them with their inadequate tools, but he applauded their idea of cutting the tree into manageable pieces and then putting it back together again. Of course, it was spurred by necessity, the mother of invention, he reflected. He was still thinking about their ingenuity when he halted, his lips parting as he stared into space. Thoughts leapfrogged, exploding in his mind, gathering their own momentum, screaming silently at him.

"*Shit!*" he bit out.

Joey stopped and stared at him. "What is it?" She frowned.

"Cutting things up to move them, then putting them back together," he flung at her, and her frown deepened. "What if you're not the only ones doing it?" he said.

"What are you talking about?" she asked.

"I'm talking about sloops being cut apart so they can be moved on small wagons and put together again afterward," he said.

She stared back as she absorbed his answer. "Put together again in caves?" she offered.

"Bull's-eye, dammit," Fargo shouted. "In caves, out of sight. Of course, that'd only be part of it, but it would explain a lot of things."

"Such as?" she questioned.

Thoughts raced through his mind, all suddenly falling into place. "Wagons small enough to get through the mountains, yet able to carry half or a quarter of a ship. Moving only by night just to play safe. Leaving tracks that didn't fit the picture," he said. "I'm going to see where those tracks really go."

"I'll come along," Joey said. He hesitated, then agreed with a nod. He didn't know what he'd find. She could be helpful. Breaking into a run, he pushed through the thick foliage and into the hollow and leaped onto the Ovaro. She fetched her short-legged horse, and he led the way back to the ledge and the wagon tracks. He followed the trail, excitement mounting, a feeling of success sweeping through him. He welcomed it, allowing himself to embrace optimism, hope, promise, until Joey said with casual matter-of-factness, "I wonder if Linda Corrigan found anything."

He reined up, his jaw dropping. "What?" he asked, shouting the question.

"Linda. I showed her the tracks," Joey said.

"Oh, damn, damn damn," Fargo exploded with a groan. "When?"

"She was here the morning after you left with Cornelia," Joey said. He groaned inwardly. The night he'd spent making love to Cornelia instead of coming back, he reminded himself. He swore again as Joey went on. "She asked what I knew about other tracks. I told her—didn't see any harm in it. Besides, I didn't expect you'd be coming back."

"Not your fault," he muttered.

"She said you'd want her to know," Joey added.

Fargo bit out an expletive. "Damn her clever bitchiness."

"I thought you two were working together," Joey said.

"Hardly," Fargo grunted.

"All she wants is to find out who killed her brother. She can't hurt you by that," Joey said.

"Hell she can't," Fargo snapped.

"How?"

"There are two ways to hurt somebody. You can do something on purpose, or you can just get in the way and cause trouble by it. She can do either," Fargo said and sent the Ovaro forward. "It's spilled milk. There's nothing to do about it now," he said, his eyes focusing on the wagon tracks that ran along the leafy lane. When they began to curve downward, he felt hope pulling at him again.

12

The forest stayed dense as Fargo followed the wagon tracks down through passages barely wide enough for them to fit. The accompanying horse fell back to ride behind and between wagons, he noted. He saw the long shadows of late afternoon begin to reach into the thick woods, and the downward slope began to level off. "Rein up," Joey suddenly said. "The caves are just ahead." He pulled the Ovaro to a halt, glanced at her, and frowned as he squinted through the thick leaves and saw only more leaves. "You come onto them all of a sudden," she said and slid from her horse.

He dismounted and walked beside her as she pushed through low branches, and suddenly he saw two of the caves appear before him, a flat, cleared area of ground in front of both, some fifty feet wide, he guessed. The first thing he spotted were the wagons lined up at the side of each cave. He had read the tracks correctly, he grunted silently. Owensboro mountain wagons with oversize brakes and high drivers' seats. A two-horse hitch on each along with a one-horse farm wagon. He draped the Ovaro's reins over a low branch and started forward on foot, scanning the huge, cavernous mouths of both caves. Drawing still closer, Joey beside him, he heard voices coming from inside the caves, then the sounds of hammering and more voices.

He glanced over the mouths of both caves and saw no guards at either, carefully went forward again, and felt Joey's touch on his arm. She gestured to the left, and he saw the third cave, thick, overhanging honey locust trees shading most of the entrance. Flickering light reached out from inside the caves. Too strong for candles, he decided. Wall torches, he murmured. Joey's voice whispered in his ear, "No guards."

"I can think of three reasons," he said, and she waited. "They're being extra careful not to draw attention to themselves, they're really well hidden, or they feel sure nobody knows about them."

"Guess that lets Linda out," Joey said.

"Why?" he asked.

"They'd have guards posted if she'd warned them or got herself caught," Joey said.

"Maybe, and maybe they're extra smart. Right now I don't even know that I'm right. I have to get a look inside those caves," he said.

"And get yourself caught while you're at it?"

"You know a better way to see what's inside?" he asked.

"Wait and see what comes out," she answered.

"Can't wait. It could be too late now. I've got to see for myself," he said and lowered his long frame to the ground as dusk began to turn to night.

"I just wait here?" Joey asked.

"For a spell. You've done enough getting me this far. I don't come out, you get the hell back home," he told her. It wasn't her fight. She had her private, mountain world. He'd no mind to make her part of another world that was perhaps no better for her, for any of them. He started to crawl forward when her face came against his, her lips pressing his.

"For luck," she murmured as she drew back. He began to crawl into the open, but stayed snail-like along the ground. The darkness deepened quickly, and the torchlight from inside the caves became more pronounced. When he reached the entrance to the first cave, he halted, his eyes searching the bushes and the trees on both sides. He saw nothing, no movement of shadowed figures, nothing. But the sounds of voices were louder, and the noise of hammers stronger. Staying flat on the ground, he moved forward into the first of the caves. Shifting direction, he crawled to the side of the cave entrance and inched forward against the rock wall.

Figures began to take shape in front of him, and he felt spiraling excitement. He saw the small sloops, three of them, each supported by a wood cradle. One was just having the stern end pushed into place beside the rest of the little ship as a crew of workmen fastened it to the main part of the hull. He squinted and saw they used nails to fasten the two sections together along with metal clamps. His eyes went to the other two cradles, the sloops inside them completely put together except for the single mast that lay beside each one.

That was the last piece to be put in place when the sloops were put into the water, he noted. He lay still, watching as the workmen hammered and pushed and others began applying a caulking compound to where the sections were joined. These sloops were not designed for a long life, obviously. They were made to sail, fire their cannons, and be sunk if need be, so long as they accomplished their mission. But he had called it right. This was the last, most important part of the entire devilishly clever operation. Yet he frowned as he began to slide backward. There were still questions open, details he had to know. Scooting back along the edge of the cave wall, he reached the entrance to the cavern, stayed flat on his stomach, and crawled to the next cave. Only a few workmen were there, most polishing masts lying on the floor of the cave beside three sloops that were put together.

Forcing himself not to grow careless, he inched his way to the next cave, where he saw only one man and two completed sloops. The last two caves held two finished sloops each and a half dozen workmen applying caulking and maneuvering a cannon into place at the rear of each cutter. At each cave he searched the deep recesses, looking for short blond hair, wondering each time if he'd find her a guest or a prisoner. But he didn't find her at all, and he finally began to push his way slowly back along the caves, flattening himself against the outer wall of one when a half dozen men walked past. He halted outside the first cave and let his breath return. Crawling was its own kind of work, he decided.

There were still major questions. The sloops that were now put back together could never be transported the rest of the way by the small mountain wagons. Yet he'd seen no other rigs. Were they still to come? he wondered. It had to be soon, real soon. They couldn't risk leaving the sloops sitting in the caves and possibly being discovered. Which meant there wasn't enough time for him to ride all the way to Washington and Cornelia, have her communicate with Stanton and assemble another force. The sloops in the caves would be somewhere in the water by tomorrow night, he was certain, and within another day, sailing the high seas to sink federal vessels.

He'd have to find a way to stop that, or everything he had uncovered would be an empty exercise. He would have found the wasps' nest, but the wasps would be gone. He'd have a hollow victory at best. Those who'd planned so cleverly and carefully would find another way through the mountains. Fargo swore, bitterly realizing the dilemma he faced. He didn't fancy hollow victories, and right now that's what stared back at him. Crawling again, he found his way back to the trees, aware that he had taken much longer than he'd expected. When he reached the trees, Joey was gone, and he was happy for that. She had followed his orders, he grunted, grateful she was safely out of the way. He retrieved the Ovaro and rode slowly, finding his way carefully through the dark denseness of the mountains.

Linda came into his thoughts, and he wondered what had become of her. Had she turned away without following the tracks to the caves? Perhaps she had decided the tracks were too small to be the right ones. He had once been convinced of that. The probability made him feel better, and his thoughts turned to the quandary that rode with him. Time had become the enemy that would rob him of victory. Only he refused to stand by helplessly and see victory vanish, not without one last try. As he picked his way through the dark, he began to form plans—wild, crazy, grasping, unworkable plans that he somehow had to make work. Time had given him no other choice. He had perhaps twenty-four hours to salvage victory, to stop the next flotilla of sea raiders from sailing.

But a starving man didn't have the luxury to pick and choose what he'd eat. He had to make do with whatever came to his plate, and, Fargo realized, he was not unlike a starving man. He couldn't pick a fine force of troopers. He couldn't choose time, position, equipment. He had to make do with what was on his plate, and that was a ragtag collection of wild mountain folk. But by the time he reached the hollow, he had his plans set. He was ready for that one last try.

The hollow was silent and sleeping, except for the kettles that bubbled continuously, and he made his way into the thick trees. Joey, obviously awake, ran from the house and threw her arms around him. "You told me not to stay," she said.

"So I did." He nodded.

"I thought something had happened to you," she said, bringing him into the house.

"No. I was lucky," Fargo said. "We have to talk. The sloops are ready for one last trip to be launched. I've got to stop that, and I'll need help . . . your mountain men. They'll do it if you tell them to."

"I wouldn't do that, but they can decide for themselves. They're always spoiling for a good fight," Joey said. "But you'll have to offer them something. They won't fight for you, or anybody, for nothing. That'd be against common sense and pride. What can you offer them? Not fancy words, fine patriotic speeches. That won't be enough."

"I didn't expect it would. I've plenty to offer them. But I'll want to be leaving first thing in the morning. Those sloops will be moving come dark. I want to be there and ready," he said.

"I'll have everyone turned out to listen," Joey said.

"Good. How many of you are there old enough to shoot and fight?" Fargo asked.

"Forty . . . fifty counting womenfolk," Joey said.

"Not counting womenfolk," he said.

"Why not? The Cole women can outshoot their men. So can the Crabble girls," Joey said. "They'd want to take part, stand beside their menfolk. Those are our ways, too."

"Whatever you say." He shrugged, felt tiredness sweep over him, and pulled off clothes and fell onto the bed. Joey came at once to sleep tight against him, and when morning came, he felt her get up. He opened his eyes and sat up as she vanished out the door. Dressing quickly, he went outside through the trees, the Ovaro at his heels, and pushed into the hollow, where he found it crowded with the mountain people, a number of them ones he'd not seen before. Joey waited near Zeke Cole.

"Told them some of it. You tell them the rest," she said. He gazed at the waiting faces and spoke quickly, no holding back, no varnishing anything. They listened, apparently unbothered by the facts he laid out before them. Zeke Cole was the first to speak when he finished.

"Sounds like it'll be a damn good fight," he said. "But we didn't hear what you're offerin' for our help."

He had taken Joey's advice and stayed away from patriotic speeches and grandiose appeals. Now he followed the same simple approach by making his offer practical, down-to-earth, and aimed at their material needs. "Pretty much anything you need or want," Fargo began, certain that John Nicolay and Cornelia would gratefully come through on anything he asked for. "Let's start with all the two-man bucking saws you'll ever need, two-man faller's crosscut saws, broadaxes, double-bit axes, new bowie knives, as many good, sound army horses as you want, heavy army coats, top-grade leather boots, and this." He halted, stepped to the Ovaro, and pulled the big Henry from its saddle case. He picked out a sapling with new, thin branches, put the rifle to his shoulder, and began firing. He fired all fifteen of its bullets without a pause and blasted away fifteen sections of tree branches. Lowering the rifle, he saw their eyes staring in awe. Not just because of his marksmanship, he knew, but because of the rifle.

"That's some kind of rifle," Elwood Crabble breathed.

"The new Henry repeating rifle," Fargo said. "There won't be a varmint you can't bring down. You can have as many as you want and the ammunition for them. All this is just for starters. You tell me what else you want, and I'll get it for you."

"I want a bathtub," Joey said.

"It's yours," Fargo answered.

"Good wool dresses and nightclothes for the young-uns," Rebecca Cole said.

"It's done," Fargo said.

"A new butter churn," Sally Crabble called out.

"Done," Fargo said.

"New sheets of tar paper and canvas, plenty of nails and hammers," Zed Crabble said.

"You've got it," Fargo said.

"As many of those Henrys as we want?" the man asked.

"That's what I said." Fargo nodded, then waited as they leaned into each other and exchanged murmured words. It was Zeke Cole who spoke for everyone.

"When do we start fightin' for you?" he asked.

"Before the day's over, so we move soon as we can," Fargo said, and let out a long sigh of relief.

"Some of us are coming along," Mary Crabble said. He nodded, glad for as much firepower as he could get. His eyes slowly scanned everyone gathered before him. Almost everyone had a hunting knife, he saw, and most held their varmint rifles. He noted a number of pistols, most Colt-Paterson old holster pistols with a few of the old-style, long-barreled Colt-Paterson single-action guns.

"There's something I have to know because we win only if we can do what I plan on doing," he said. "How many of you have bows and arrows?"

"Everybody does. We use 'em often, specially for wild turkey. Saves digging lead out of a bird," Zeke Cole answered.

"Get your bows and your arrows," Fargo said, then focused on the women. "I'll need strips of cloth, all you can give me," he said. "And whatever grease or fat you can give me."

"Wheel grease and plenty of hog fat," one of the Dorrance women said.

"That'll do," he said, then waited till the others returned with their bows and arrows, a few long bows, but mostly short sinew-backed weapons. "I came here from the Western territories," he said. "It seems only right that I take a page from the Cheyenne, the Kiowa, the Sioux, the Crow, and all the other Plains tribes." As the women returned with the strips of cloth, everyone crowded closer as Fargo showed them how to prepare fire arrows by wrapping the cloth around the arrow just back of the arrowhead, then coating the small ball of material with grease. After he'd done three, he had some of the others do the rest until at least a dozen were finished. "Comes the right time, you light them and let fly," Fargo said. "I'll give you

the exact time and spot later. Now let's get moving."
He turned as the others dispersed, those who were
going with him lining up at one side of the hollow.
Joey stood beside him as he swung onto the Ovaro.
"Too bad we don't have many horses. We'll be
slowed down this way," he said.

"No we won't," she said. "They'll make as good
time on foot through these mountains as you will."

She swung onto her short-legged horse, and Fargo
went to the head of the column, glanced back, and
saw not more than four or five on horseback. He
waved, started forward, and Joey came up to ride beside him. In only a few minutes they were in the deep
denseness of the high ledge, once again following the
tracks. As he rode in silence, he glanced to each side
and caught glimpses of flitting figures that wove in
and out of the thick tree growths like so many shadows—not unlike Indian warriors. He smiled and
thought about the fire arrows he'd made. There was
nothing wrong in borrowing from old foes. He was
getting to feel more at home.

The thick wooded terrain refused to yield, and the
hours seemed to drag on. The day was starting to
wind itself to an end when the trail turned downward
and Fargo hurried the pinto forward. When the slope
began to level off, he saw the wall of oaks rising
ahead, recognized the spot, and knew the trees would
abruptly halt. He reined up, waved an arm, and the
figures materialized out of the forest, Zeke Cole and
Elwood Crabble in the forefront. Fargo dismounted,
reached into his saddlebag, and brought out a dozen

lucifers, which he handed to the others. "Light your arrows only when you're ready to fire," he said.

"When will that be?" Zeke Cole asked.

"When you hear my first shot," Fargo said. "From here on, you spread out behind me. We'll stop when we can see the caves. From what I saw, there'll be only the workmen, a handful of guards on horseback, and the drivers on the wagons." He paused, and his lips tightened. He wanted his ragtag little army to do what he'd brought them to do. He'd ask nothing more of them. They weren't equipped for more. He wanted no heroics from them that would only result in their slaughter. "Being honest, my friends, I can't be sure what's waiting for us. If they surprise us with a major force, after we hit them, then you break off, run, vanish into the mountains the way you do and go home. Your job will be over."

"What about you?" Joey asked.

"My neck, my problem. I expect I'll get out of it," he said.

Her arms circled his neck. "Come back," she said.

"Have to. Got a delivery to make." He smiled, stepped back, and swung onto the pinto again. "Let's go, slow and silent," he said and walked the horse forward, glimpsed the others moving forward as they spread out on both sides of him, weapons in hand. The time had come to retrieve victory, to make it real instead of hollow.

13

When the caves came into sight, dusk had begun to filter through the mountain foliage, and Fargo called a halt, his eyes narrowing as he swept the area in front of the caves. Grim satisfaction coursed through him. He'd guessed right about everything, their timetable and the giant rigs that were lined up in front of the caves, ready to roll as night drew closer. No mountain wagons now. These were massive, extended logging rigs with forty-inch-high wheels and four-inch-wide tires. Each had been outfitted with high sides and entirely wrapped in canvas, each able to haul a complete, put-together sloop. He took note of a long timber wagon at the rear of the others, heavy rolled canvas concealing the masts wrapped inside it.

He paused at the ten guards on horseback who were lined up alongside the six huge logging trucks, letting his eyes travel down the fairly steep slope in front of the waiting caravan. He leaned to Joey beside him. "What river is waiting for them when they reach bottom?" he asked.

"The James," she said.

"Which would let them sail right down to Hampton Roads and the Atlantic after they launch the sloops," Fargo grunted. "Only they'll never get that far." The creak of wagon wheels sounded as the last of the day began to fade, and Fargo saw the first of the big logging rigs begin to roll. The others followed after it, the guards spread out in a thin line beside them as they nosed down the slope, each big rig drawn by a four-horse team. He moved forward, raised one arm, and the others turned their eyes to him. They saw him draw the big Henry from its saddle case and raise it to his shoulder. "Light your arrows and pick your wagons," he said, and waited, the rifle aimed, his finger on the trigger. He waited another thirty seconds, watching the lead wagon start down the slope, a figure beside the driver working the extra-long-handled brake. Suddenly, he felt what he waited for, the heat of the flames erupting from the fire arrows.

He fired a single shot first, then four more in quick succession and saw three of the guards topple from their horses as if they'd all been pulled by an invisible string. The others reined up as the trees erupted in a fusillade of gunfire. At the same instant a hail of flaming arrows arced through the air and slammed into the wagons. The weathered canvas burst into flames at once, and Fargo gave a shout of triumph. Canvas and underneath it, newly varnished wood, perfect fuel for voracious flames.

He saw the rest of the guards go down in the second volley of gunfire from the trees, and now, with frightening fury, every wagon was a rolling fireball.

Fargo burst into the open as he saw the drivers struggling to control their teams that were galloping down the slope. But it was a futile struggle as the horses, panicked by the roaring flames that followed close behind them, raced down the slope, totally out of control. They careened around curves too fast, striking uneven ground at breakneck speed as the flames leaped and whistled through the night. Fargo sent the Ovaro after the caravan of flames and terror-stricken horses, then saw the lead wagon pull into a curve, slam against a tree, and splinter into flying balls of fire as the horses raced on alone. The second huge rig simply skidded sideways into more trees and burst apart. Fargo glimpsed the burning hull of a sloop thrown into the air, and he heard the sounds of the other wagons going over, smashing into each other, horses screaming as they broke loose. He reined up and looked back at a scene of furiously burning sections of wagon and smashed ships that lit up the slope with an eerie, unreal glow.

He turned to peer back through the night at the trees, searched, and picked out figures caught by the light when an explosion of hoofbeats filled the night. He whirled and saw the riders galloping toward him from the bottom of the slope, materializing out of the darkness as they neared the fires. He cursed, wheeled the Ovaro around as he saw at least twenty riders, then started to cut to his right when six more horsemen charged out of the dark at him. Turning again, he met another six coming in from his left.

With another curse he reined up as he saw he was trapped.

The riders surrounded him, all young, all of a cut, all handling their horses with military precision. Others came up and formed a second line around him. All wore dark shirts, he noted. One moved his horse forward. "I'll take that handgun," he said. Fargo unholstered the Colt and gave it to him.

"You had to be nearby," Fargo said.

"Just down the slope," the man said. "We were on our way to meet the wagons."

"Seems you're a little late," Fargo said dryly.

"Yes, goddammit," another voice said, and Fargo saw a horseman push through the others and come up to face him, a small, dapper figure with sharply pressed shirt and trousers. The man nonetheless exuded an unmistakable air of command. "You're Fargo, of course," the little man said.

Fargo felt a frown sweep across his brow. "That more than a lucky guess?" he asked.

"You've been a thorn in our side ever since you arrived," the man said. "We didn't have to guess that you might be heading an attack on our wagons." Fargo turned the answer in his mind and was unsatisfied, but set his dissatisfaction aside for the moment. "We thought an attack would come when the ships were being put into the water. It seemed the most vulnerable moment," the man said.

"It would have been," Fargo agreed, "if I hadn't called on some old enemies."

The man's eyes scanned the still-burning pieces of

ships and wagons, his lips pulling back in distaste as he snapped orders at his men. "He didn't do this alone. Get into the trees and find the others," he said, and all but six of the horsemen immediately set off to search the trees in front of the caves. Fargo kept the grimace from his face and hoped his instructions had been followed. He studied the dapper little man in front of him for a moment. "You know me. I don't know you," he said.

"General Pierre Gustave Toutant Beauregard," the man said with a bow of his head. "Not that it matters to you. I've come to admire your abilities, Fargo. It's too bad our meeting will be such a short one."

"You telling me something?" Fargo asked mildly.

"I'm afraid so." The general smiled. "We'll be taking you to our headquarters for questioning. When we're finished, there'll be a firing squad."

"The last trail."

"Exactly."

Fargo shrugged, and his eyes went to the riders as they returned. "Nobody. Not a soul," one of the men said to the general. General Beauregard's lips thinned, and he scanned the still-burning fires with distaste.

"Most unfortunate. A real tragedy," he muttered.

"Depends where you're sitting," Fargo put in.

The general shot him a scathing glance and put his horse into a trot. Six riders surrounded Fargo and shepherded him along as the general led the way down the slope. They finally reached the rolling land at the bottom, crossed wide Virginia fields, stayed on roads where they met no one, and finally turned into a farm field, where Fargo saw a knot of men and horses. A big farmhouse rose up behind the horses with three outbuildings nearby.

"Headquarters?" Fargo asked.

"No, you've another day to live. This is one of our operations bases," the general said. "You'll stay here overnight. My men rode all day yesterday to get here. They're tired. We'll go on to headquarters in the morning. I'm going on ahead, and they'll bring you tomorrow." He turned to one of his men. "Lock him up," he said, turned, and rode away.

"Off your horse," one of his captors said, and Fargo dismounted and was led past where the others were tethering their mounts. He took note as one of the men put the Ovaro in with the other horses, and as he scanned the line of horses, an oath exploded silently. His eyes stared at the gray mare tethered at the end of one length of rope. "Let's go, let's go," the man muttered and pushed him along. He was taken to one of the smaller outbuildings, where he saw two rifle-bearing guards outside the door. They stepped aside as the four men pushed Fargo into the building, a bunkhouse with six cots inside it, he saw. The figure rose from the last cot as the men entered, and Fargo peered at the short blond hair and the deep blue eyes. "You got company tonight," one of the men said, and Fargo took in the ropes that bound Linda's wrists and ankles.

She stared at him as the men tied him ankle and wrist, arms pulled behind his back, and pushed him onto the cot next to her. "Don't take advantage of the

217

lady," one of the men said, and the others joined in his laugh as they trooped from the building, slamming the door shut behind them.

Fargo met the shock in her eyes. "How long have you been here?" he asked.

"A few days," Linda said. "I found the caves, and they found me. Been here ever since." He leaned over and peered at the marks on her wrists where she had pulled against the ropes to try to get free. "Don't you believe me?" she asked.

"I'm not sure of anything about you," he said, but he'd seen that the rope marks were at least three days old and that she had struggled to free herself. He sat at the edge of the cot, and his thoughts tumbled. Linda had blundered onto their operation, still on her search for the truth about Kenny's death. He glared at her. "You're still a pain in the ass. I'm sure about that," he said. "And that you didn't hear a damn thing about Kenny."

She glared back. "They never heard of Kenny. Neither did the general," she said.

"That figures. He's a different part of this. Kenny was killed on orders from somebody who's on top of everything," Fargo said.

"But you couldn't tell me," Linda said.

"I don't know," he said.

"You won't be telling me anything now."

"Don't be too sure of that."

"They're going to kill you. And me, just in case I know something," she said.

"I told you to go home, leave this alone. You

wouldn't listen," he reminded her. "But I'm going to give you another chance."

She uttered an incredulous laugh. "How are you going to do that? You can't give yourself another chance."

He flexed his arms and tried to let muscles bulge and loosen wrist ropes. He tried to curl his fingers back to touch the ropes, pull on them. But they had tied him expertly. He couldn't bend his arms enough to reach the calf holster around his leg. They'd overlooked it, but they might just as well have taken it. He let his thoughts go back to General Beauregard. His men had ridden hard all day to position themselves at the right place in time. That was important. That said something. But he had to fit it in place, make it part of a whole. And he hadn't time for that now. Getting free was the only thing that mattered now. Putting things together would be so much useless information in front of a firing squad.

He glanced at Linda. She sat quietly, despondently, her face drawn. He moved to reach her, came close when the ankle ropes stopped him. She looked up, a bitter smile suddenly touching her lips. "Trying for a last kiss?" she asked.

"Not a bad idea," he said.

She swung herself around. "I can meet you halfway," she said, and her bonds let her come forward enough to reach him, her lips touching his. Suddenly, he pulled back, his eyes growing wide. "I do something wrong?" she asked.

"No, Jesus, you did something right. I've a knife in a

calf holster around my right leg. I can't reach it, but you can," he said. He turned and brought his bound legs up to her. "You turn around now, back up to me, and you can pull the knife out." Understanding, she turned, brought her hands to his legs, used her fingers to slowly pull the trouser bottoms up, then found the calf holster. "Slowly now. Just pull it out, hold it until I can take it from you." He felt her fingers sliding along the calf holster, find the hilt of the thin, double-edged blade, and slowly lift it from the leather holster.

As soon as she had the blade in her fingers and clear of his trouser leg, he swung around again, backed his hands to hers, and carefully closed his fingers around the blade. When he grasped it firmly, he pulled it from her, and she moved away. He heard the breath rush from her lips. Holding the double-edged blade in his fingers, he began to saw against his wrist ropes. He had to halt every few minutes as his fingers cramped, and he waited until muscles relaxed enough for him to go on. "Can I do some?" Linda asked. "I'll be working backward, but I can try."

"No," he said. "If we drop it, we're finished altogether."

"Don't even think that," she murmured as he continued his torturous sawing, little strokes, stopping, waiting, sawing again. But suddenly he felt the rope give, and he renewed efforts, fighting away the pain of cramped fingers when suddenly the rope parted. With a cry of pain and triumph combined, he pulled his hands free, let his fingers uncramp, and rubbed circulation back in his wrists. He cut his ankle bonds, then turned to Linda, severing her ropes with a few quick strokes of the knife. She rose, swayed for a moment, then steadied herself.

"I want a promise from you," he said. "I get you out of here, you're going home, back to your plants. I'll find out who's responsible for Kenny's death. When I do, I'll tell you. No promise and I leave you here."

"You wouldn't do that," she said with total confidence, and he silently swore at her.

"How'd they let you go to the bathroom?" he asked.

"I called, and the guards came, untied me, and took me to the outhouse," Linda said.

"Sit down as if you were tied and call them," he said, then crossed the room in four long steps to stand beside the door. Linda called out, and in moments the door opened and one of the guards stepped into the room. He started across the room when Fargo smashed him on the back of the neck with a tremendous blow. The man started to collapse, but Fargo caught him and pulled him out of sight behind the half-open door. Fargo waited in a crouch, his knife in his hand this time. It took a moment, but the second guard finally called out. "Jeremy, you all right?" he asked. When his only answer was silence, he hurried into the room, a rifle in his hands. Fargo sprang from behind the door and pressed the point of the blade into the man's neck.

"Drop the gun, or you're a dead man," he said. The man let the rifle fall to the floor. As soon as the gun left his hands, Fargo swung him around and sank a blow into the man's belly. The man doubled over and fell to his knees. He was still on his knees when Fargo brought the stock of the rifle down on his head and the man pitched forward onto his face and lay still. Fargo rose, beckoned to Linda who was at his side instantly, then stepped from the building with her. There was almost no moon, barely enough for them to see their way, and Fargo moved in a crouch, Linda staying close, and found where the horses were tethered. He moved among the horses and came upon the Ovaro first, then saw his Colt and the big Henry were with the horse, the Colt stuck into the rifle case. He found the gray mare next, and Linda swung onto the horse as he led the Ovaro out of the area.

He moved quietly behind the tethered horses, saw clumps of sleeping figures dotting the ground, kept away from each, and finally had cleared the area. He climbed onto the Ovaro and fastened a hard stare at Linda. "I'm going to get my things at the house first," she said. "When will you be paying me a visit in the Blue Ridge?"

"Whenever." He shrugged.

"You didn't come to rescue me, but thanks anyway," she said.

"I just hope I didn't make a mistake," he growled.

"Forget the thanks," she snapped and sent the mare into a canter. He turned the Ovaro northeast in the dark night and rode without hurrying. He wanted the time to try to put pieces together, and he wasn't at all sure he could. Or that he'd like the answer if he did.

14

Exhaustion demanded that he rest some, so Fargo pulled under a thick-branched shagbark hickory and gave himself a few hours sleep. When he woke, the day had turned gray and misty, and he reached Washington in midafternoon. The day had grown grayer, the mist turning to fog, and he rode directly to Cornelia's house. Surprise swept over him when he saw three carriages lined up at the curb and four army troopers standing guard at the door. Frowning, he dismounted, and one of the troopers barred his way as he strode to the front door. "Skye Fargo to see Miss Jeffers," he said. The soldier went into the house, then reappeared a moment later with Captain Winslow and John Nicolay at his heels.

Both men wore tight, strained faces. "Come in, Fargo. Thank God you're here," Nicolay said.

"You're looking real troubled, both of you," Fargo said as he walked into the house with the two men.

"More than troubled. Devastated," Nicolay said.

"This ought to help. The last shipment of sloops has

been destroyed, and it's not likely they'll be making any more," Fargo said.

Both men's eyes widened. "By God, that is great news, Fargo, simply wonderful news," Captain Winslow said. "Your doing, I take it."

"More or less. Had some help," Fargo said.

"The president will be giving you a medal for this," John Nicolay said. "Unfortunately, our news is what has devastated us. They've taken Cornelia."

Fargo stared at both men. "Taken her?" he echoed. "Who?"

"Secessionist forces, of course. They apparently found out she was working for us, and they've taken her. They'll no doubt treat her as a spy, and you know what that means," Nicolay said.

Fargo's lips pursed as thoughts tumbled through his mind. It was a development he hadn't expected, and he almost smiled at the bold cleverness of it. "When did this happen?" he asked.

"This morning," the president's secretary said.

"How do you know this?" Fargo pressed.

Captain Winslow answered. "One of my men saw it happen. Four men had her between them and hurried her into a carriage, a closed coupe with windows drawn. Everything about it told him something was wrong, and he had his horse and followed the carriage. It took her to the Potomac, where a small sailboat waited. The four men took her aboard and sailed off."

"Your man couldn't follow any farther?" Fargo asked.

"Actually, he did. He found a fisherman in a dory, paid the man to row after them. The fog was already coming up, though not as blanketing as it is now, and the fisherman was able to follow until the sailboat headed into deep waters. He refused to go any farther, then rowed my man back to shore and left him there."

"Then you don't really know what's happened to Cornelia," Fargo said.

"Oh, it's quite obvious. They want her completely away, where there's no chance any of our people could get to her or see her. There's a British merchantman, the *Neptune*, anchored off the mouth of the bay. That's where they've taken her," Winslow said.

"They've sailed by now," Fargo said with a silent curse.

"No. The fog is thick as pea soup, and there's no wind. There are at least ten ships in the area, all becalmed, including one of ours. Nobody will be moving until the fog lifts and the wind comes up. That probably won't be till the morning," the captain said.

"When that happens, you can go after her," Fargo said.

Winslow wrinkled his brow. "Unfortunately, the *Neptune* is the fastest vessel out there, a four-masted bark that'll outrun any of us. When the wind comes up, there'll be no catching her," the captain said.

"Then I'll get to her while everyone's still fogbound, but I'm getting to her," Fargo said.

"It'll be night in another hour. You'll never find her in fog so thick you can hardly see your hand in front of your face, not among all those other ships," Winslow said.

"There must be a way. Get me out there, and I'll get aboard and come back with Cornelia," Fargo said.

"Just take her off the *Neptune* under the noses of the entire crew?" Winslow said.

"I've done as much. I can do it again. The fog and the sea are my real problem," Fargo said. "That's your department. Find a way to get me out there."

Winslow frowned into space, muttering aloud, as much to himself as to Fargo. "Jack Kiley. Maybe Jack Kiley," he said.

"Who's Jack Kiley?" Fargo questioned.

"A seaman, a bosun's mate. It's positively uncanny what he can hear. You might call him a seagoing trailsman. The way you read signs on land, distinguish sounds, pick out marks, features, prints, the way you read tracks, leaves, trees, all of nature, he does at sea, only with ships, seabirds, waves."

"Where is he?"

"At our station on the lower Potomac."

"Get him. I'm taking Cornelia off that ship," Fargo said.

"Stay here, rest some. I'll need a few hours," Winslow said and strode from the house. Fargo turned to Nicolay.

"I could use some coffee and a sandwich," Fargo said. Nicolay relayed the request to a servant nearby, then turned back, his face still grave.

"We haven't told you the rest. Our intelligence tells

us an attempt to assassinate the president is planned," Nicolay said.

"No idea of where, when, or how, of course," Fargo said.

"No, not yet. But we know there are those who feel that with Mister Lincoln gone there'd be no need for secession. They feel lesser men could come to lesser solutions," Nicolay said.

"What does the president think?" Fargo asked.

"He feels he must go his course and depend on our people to protect him," Nicolay said. "But it's clear that our people have been compromised. They tell us their movements are known to the other side before they're made. Now with Cornelia gone, we've lost our most valuable operative."

"I'm bringing back Cornelia," Fargo said, his voice suddenly hard.

"I hope you can. You've already done your job. We can't ask you to do more, but that's what I'm doing," Nicolay said.

"Let's say it's personal. Cornelia's beauty can make a man do most anything. It stays, hangs on," Fargo said, hesitating, then decided not to say anything more, not even to John Nicolay, not till he had Cornelia back. The servant came back with a beef sandwich for him and a shot of good bourbon. He ate in the study and napped on the thick couch. Night had descended when he woke, heard the voices from outside, and went into the main room of the house. Winslow was there with a smallish man in a bosun's uniform, a pleasant, ruddy face, and sharp eyes, hair with a red tinge.

"Fargo, this is bosun's mate Jack Kiley. I told him about you on the way here. He's promised to do his best for you," the captain said.

Jack Kiley looked a little shy. "From what I hear about you, Fargo, I'm an amateur," he said.

"This is your home ground, Jack. I'm the amateur here," Fargo said. "You get me to the right place. I'll make the rest happen."

"There's a coupe and driver and two fast horses waiting outside. They'll take you to a light dory at Newport News," Captain Winslow said.

"Let's go." Fargo nodded and went outside with the little bosun, stopped at the Ovaro, and took the rifle. Jack Kiley sat quietly beside him as the driver of the coupe let the horses go full out. Fargo peered through the thickness of the fog, which had only grown thicker as they came closer to their destination. They were nearing Newport News when Jack Kiley spoke.

"There are some things you'd best know," he said. "Most of the ships beyond the bay will keep a fore and aft lantern on, maybe a top-deck light, and a port and starboard lantern. In this fog all you'll see is a glow, if that. I won't be looking. I'll be listening mostly."

"Is that how you'll find the *Neptune*?" Fargo asked.

"Yes. Like you, I've learned to see with my ears," Kiley said. "Every kind of ship has its own voice. They speak with everything that's on them and part of them—their rigging, their lanyards, stays and shrouds, halyards, blocks and beckets, their sails and spars. They speak in the way the sea hits their hulls, even when they're anchored, certainly when they're moving. Most seamen pay no attention to those things, but I have, just as you know a raccoon sounds different going through a forest than a chipmunk, a wolf different than a fox. A square-rigger sounds very different from a topsail schooner. Water against the hull of a staysail schooner sends a very different sound than water against a full-rigged ship."

"I'd guess it takes a lot more listening than it does in the forest," Fargo said.

"It's probably trickier, but then there aren't as many sounds to distract a body," the bosun said and broke off as the carriage came to a halt. With a quick, lithe movement he was outside, standing at the edge of a low dock in the fog. Fargo followed as the little man somehow found the dory, stepped in it, and sat down at the oars.

"I can give a hand rowing," Fargo said.

"Good. We've a fair piece of water to cross before we reach the mouth of the bay," Jack Kiley said, making room on the wooden center seat for Fargo. Taking hold of the right oar, Fargo quickly fell into rhythm with Kiley's long stroke. The fog surrounded them, and Fargo felt as though he rowed suspended in space. Kiley, hardly visible next to him, continued to set a steady pace.

"How the hell do you know we're going in the right direction?" Fargo asked.

"Hold your oar up," Kiley said, and Fargo lifted his oar out of the water. "Listen to the water slap against the boat," Kiley said. Fargo listened and heard the small, slapping sound of the water.

"It's hitting straight against the bow," he said.

"That's right. There's almost no wind, which means the water's coming straight in from the mouth of the bay and the sea behind it. We're exactly on course," the bosun said. Fargo returned his oar to the water and rowed with Kiley and found himself wondering again if the little man was right, as there seemed no end to the sea and fog. But suddenly Fargo caught a glow spreading through the fog. Kiley pulled his oar out of the water completely. "We'll paddle from here. No sound of wood against wood," he said. "Every ship will have someone on fog watch, listening more than looking."

Fargo paddled with his oar silently dipping into the sea and felt almost as though he were back on a lake, paddling a canoe silently past a Sioux encampment. Another glow of yellowish light filtered through the fog, closer, and he saw Jack Kiley incline his head, listening. Fargo could hear the creak of the ship that rode up and down in the water, and he heard ropes pulling against each other. "Three-masted fore-and-aft schooner," Kiley said, paddling on. Another glow of light came through the fog, to their right, reddish in color. "Port light," Kiley said, and swung closer. They passed the foggy glow, and again he saw Kiley listening. Fargo strained his ears and caught the sound of the vessel as it gently rolled in the water. "A ketch," Kiley said. "She's almost bobbin' in the water."

They paddled on, and the next glow of fog-bound light came from almost directly in front of them, as diffused as the others had been, but larger, spreading farther in the fog. Kiley stopped paddling, listened, and Fargo did the same, found himself feeling proud as he distinguished the sound of the hidden ship from the others they had passed. "It's got a heavier creak to it," Fargo said.

"Aye," Jack Kiley said. "You've a good ear. Every spar is bigger, heavier. She's a square-rigger, probably a four-master, a big, heavy vessel. Every mast creaks the same. That's the way she's rigged." He bent to paddling again, and they went on without hearing another vessel or seeing another glow until suddenly Kiley held his hand up and halted the little boat. "Listen," he said. Fargo leaned forward and suddenly heard the sound of the ship directly ahead of them.

He heard the sound of halyards stretching, rubbing, the soft sound of blocks being pulled, a quiet groaning. He managed to see Jack Kiley's face as the man leaned forward, listening, his lips drawn back. Kiley was hearing subtleties that escaped him, Fargo knew, distinguishing one creak from another, interpreting each groan of rope and wood. "Square-rigger, but with staysails, lighter shrouds, and a stern spanker. That's her, a full-rigged bark," he said.

"Why no running lights or fog lights?" Fargo asked.

"They're taking no chances. They're staying hidden in every way they can. They wouldn't be doing that for ordinary passengers," Kiley said. "You'll probably find small cabin or deck lights aboard her, where you can't see them from off ship."

He began to paddle, and Fargo joined in until the dark bulk loomed up in front of them, and Kiley called a stop to paddling, letting the forward motion of the dory carry them to the ship. The fog suddenly lifted ever so slightly, and Fargo felt a soft puff of breeze. The shrouded bulk took on shape, a long hull that seemed to evaporate as quickly as it had appeared. But they were almost against the side of the ship, and using his paddle, Fargo brought the nose of the dory soundlessly against the hull. "Put your paddle down and get in the bow," Kiley said, and Fargo scrambled forward, reached out, and put his hands against the hull of the ship. "Feel along the hull. You ought to come to a Jacob's ladder," Jack Kiley whispered.

"What's that?" Fargo returned.

"A rope ladder hanging down from the deck rail. They'll probably have one in place in this fog, or they ought to," Kiley said. Fargo, using his hands, moved the dory along the long side of the vessel and suddenly stopped as he felt the rope ladder against the hull. He'd no need for the rifle, and he left it in the boat as he swung onto the rope rung of the ladder.

"You stay here," he said to Jack Kiley.

"Didn't figure to do anything else," the bosun said.

Fargo began to climb up the rope ladder, saw the rail materialize when he was almost on it, carefully climbed over it, and sank to the deck. The ship was still shrouded in fog, and he could hardly see the bottom of the nearest huge mast. But a small, diffused smear of light beckoned to him from down in the stern. He crept toward it on silent, careful steps, not only because he could see very little, but because he heard a cough and then footsteps to his right. The footsteps were joined by another pair.

"You hear anything, mate?" a voice said.

"Thought I did," the other voice said, and both fell silent. The men were some twenty feet from him along the opposite rail, he guessed. "Damn fog plays tricks on a man," one voice said trailing away. Fargo continued on toward the smear of light. It became a lantern when he reached it, and the fog spread apart enough for him to see he was at a stern cabin, a hatchway open in front of him. He stepped into it, went down a few steps where the fog didn't penetrate, and saw the door to the cabin. He closed his left hand around the doorknob, carefully turned, and the door opened. A very small candle burned in the cabin, and he saw the figure asleep on the bunk bed, the flickering candlelight catching the full, brilliant flame hair. She wore a thin white nightgown, slept half on her side, and one luscious, creamy breast escaped the top of the gown.

He was across the small cabin in two silent steps, staring down at the beauty of her with awe he realized would never leave him. He put one hand over her lovely mouth and pressed lightly. Cornelia's eyes snapped open and stared at him, fright the first emotion in the agate green orbs. Surprise followed, and she started to push up from the bunk bed. He drew his hand back as she sat up, eyes still wide with surprise. "Get dressed. We're leaving. I'm taking you off here," he said.

Her lips fell open as she stared at him. "It's suicide. They have lookouts across the entire ship," Cornelia said.

"I got in here. I'll get you out," Fargo said.

"You managed to get through alone. You'll never get off taking me. Don't get yourself killed. It's bad enough one of us has to die," she said, her hands coming up to rest against his chest, pleading in her eyes. "I can't let you do this for me, Fargo," she said.

"Get dressed," he hissed. She stepped back and pulled off the nightgown as he drank in her voluptuousness. She dressed in a shirt and Levi's and put her bag around her neck by its long strap. He took her arm and crossed the cabin to the door, listened for a second, and then pushed out into the narrow hatchway. He took the three steps up to the deck as a gust of wind met him, and he stopped as though he'd been struck. Another gust blew into his face. "Shit," he hissed as he peered out of the hatchway. The fog hadn't lifted yet, but it was moving, separating as if it were a huge, fuzzy blanket being slowly pulled apart.

The stern of the deck was still enshrouded, but when the wind gusted, he caught a glimpse of a lookout amidships as the fog rolled away for a moment. Another stretch of fog thinned, and he saw another armed lookout alongside the ship's rail. The wind was strengthening, and he saw the fog beginning to pull apart in more places, hanging in the air some six or seven feet above the deck, and he glimpsed winches, bollards, capstans. The Jacob's ladder had been somewhere amidship, he guessed, but there was no time for searching as the fog parted again, swept back, and separated once more. "Come on," he said, and pulled her by the hand. She ran with him as he headed for a stretch of rail when suddenly he felt her falling, going down head first. She screamed as she hit the deck, and he stopped, spun, and saw her on her hands and knees.

But he heard the shouts erupt from all parts of the long ship. Cornelia looked up at him. "Go, save yourself," she said, but he reached down, yanked her to her feet, and pulled her with him, reaching the rail as a bank of fog swirled away. He glanced back and saw at least eight figures running across the deck toward him. He grabbed Cornelia, swung her into the air, and, still holding her, pulled one long leg over the top of the wide wooden rail. A shot rang out, then another, whistling past him. He flung Cornelia over the side and watched her tumble through the air as she screamed. He was over the rail, leaping from the ship as she hit the water with a loud splash. He landed a few feet from her, knifed through the water for a second, and instantly pushed to the surface.

Cornelia floated less than two feet away, a glaze over her eyes. She had hit the water on her back, the hard shock of it still on her, and he came around, put one arm around her from the rear, and started to swim with her. A volley of shots hit the water all around him with a plinking sound, and, cursing, he plunged under the surface with Cornelia. He swam underwater, but he knew Cornelia hadn't taken in a deep breath, and he had to surface seconds after. He kicked, broke into the air, and heard Cornelia gag and spit out water. A quick glance showed him her eyes had cleared.

"Swim," he hissed and released his hold on her. She turned and went with him as he struck out. But another volley of bullets slammed into the water, each sending up a tiny spray. "Down," he said, going under, treading water in place until he saw her come down beside him. She swam alongside him until he surfaced and came up gasping with him. The shots had stopped, and the fog lay in long patches atop the water. Jack Kiley had to have heard the shouts and shots as well as the two loud splashes when Cornelia and he hit the water, Fargo knew, and he squinted through the dawn light for the dory. He saw nothing and cursed as the fog rolled in, blotting out any chance to see the boat. He tread water, unwilling to swim too far away. Kiley wasn't the kind to run. He was somewhere, searching also. But another sound came, and Fargo listened, frowning, then cursed. Voices sounded, then the rasp of a crank, the scrape of ropes, davits lowering a boat.

The wind was freshening with the dawn, the fog pulling apart more quickly now, and he continued to tread water as his eyes swept the patchy mist. A break opened in a bank of fog, and the dory pushed its way through, Jack Kiley still paddling with one oar.

"Here," Fargo shouted, raised an arm, and frantically waved. Kiley saw him, changed direction, and paddled toward him. Fargo cast a glance at Cornelia. She nodded at him, then followed as he swam to meet the dory. Fog trailed them as they reached the boat, and Jack Kiley leaned over, helping pull Cornelia into the dory as Fargo climbed in over the stern.

But another patch of fog blew away, and the big bark came into view, the ship's boat moving from it holding four oarsmen and four riflemen. Jack Kiley took the center seat, closed his hands over both oars, and began rowing as hard as he could after turning the dory around. But the others had seen them and were coming fast. "I'll never outrun them, lad," Jack Kiley said. "Not four oarsmen."

"Keep a straight line," Fargo said as he picked up the Henry, crawled to the stern of the boat, and flattened himself against the transom. He brought the rifle to his shoulder, waited, and saw the first volley of shots from the pursuing boat. They fell short, and Fargo took aim. The Henry could shoot farther and faster than the rifles the pursuers were using. His finger tightened on the trigger, and the rifle barked, five quick shots and three of the oarsmen fell backward into the bottom of the boat. "That'll even the match," Fargo said and saw Jack Kiley grin. Another volley of shots came from the pursuing boat, and all fell short again. Fargo glanced back, and saw a bank of fog rolling in, seconds from engulfing them. He fired two quick shots, and one of the riflemen in the other boat spun as he toppled over the side. The fog swept over the dory, hiding it from the pursuers, and Fargo saw Jack Kiley change direction.

But the fog wasn't so heavy any longer, and Fargo could see everyone in the dory with ease. Cornelia sat in the bow, her feature-perfect face drained, yet the beauty of it untouched. "By God, I think we did it," Kiley said as he continued to pull hard on the oars. Fargo's eyes searched through the fog as he peered astern, his face tight, showing neither elation nor triumph. The fog swept upward after another five minutes, and Fargo scanned the open waters, and found the sweeping lines of the big bark now in the distance, the small boat moving toward it, the pursuit over. He allowed himself a deep sigh and clambered back from the stern of the dory, sat down beside Kiley, and began to row.

Cornelia's agate green eyes stayed on him, and she formed her lips into a kiss. "I'll say everything later," she said softly. He nodded, smiled back, and bent to his rowing. The sun had come out when the dory nosed into Chesapeake Bay and Newport News. Kiley rowed to a particular pier where three carriages rested, all wearing the navy seal.

"You'll be wanting to get back to Washington," he said as Fargo helped Cornelia out of the dory, the rifle in his other hand.

"Yes, and a blanket for the lady," Fargo said.

"Be back in a minute," Kiley said, and hurried into a building, returning soon after with blanket and a young lieutenant in a crisp uniform.

"Bosun Kiley's explained everything to me. That

first carriage will take you back. I understand Captain Winslow is still in the capital," the officer said, saluted, and left. Jack Kiley took Fargo's outstretched hand.

"A fine job well done," Fargo said. "Look me up if you come West. We could make a fine team." The little bosun laughed, and Fargo wrapped the blanket around Cornelia as they climbed into the carriage. "Washington, fast as you can," he told the driver and sat back beside Cornelia, letting the warmth of the sun through the small carriage window help dry his clothes. He put his head back and closed his eyes, nestling the big Henry against one arm.

"Tired?" Cornelia asked, and linked her arm in his. "I'd imagine you must be. Want to sleep?"

"Mind if I do?" he asked.

"No, I'd like you to. I'll nap along. My night's sleep was interrupted, if you remember," she said.

"Believe I do," he said, smiled, and closed his eyes, letting the rhythm of the carriage soothe him. His eyes stayed closed, but he didn't sleep. A troubled soul never slept well, somebody had once told him. They were right, he muttered silently.

15

Day had turned to night by the time they reached Washington, and the carriage drew up before Cornelia's town house. The soldiers were gone, as were the official carriages, and he paused at the Ovaro still tethered at the hitching post, put the rifle into its saddle case, and hurried into the house after Cornelia. Two of the servants had rushed out, greeting her with excitement. "I'm fine," Cornelia told them, a little impatiently, Fargo noted.

"Mr. Nicolay left orders for someone to go to his place if you come back," one of the servants said.

"Yes, that's a good idea," Fargo said. "He say where he'd be?"

"With the president," the man said.

"We'll tell him tomorrow. There's no need for a lot of fuss over this," Cornelia cut in.

"Send someone to fetch Mister Nicolay," Fargo said with quiet firmness, and the man hurried away. Fargo saw Cornelia's eyes on him, her smile edged with ice.

"I usually give the orders in my house, Fargo," she said. "It's bad form coming from someone else."

"Indulge me. It's been an unusual time," Fargo said, and followed her into the bedroom, where she pulled off still damp clothes, disappeared into the bathroom, and returned wearing a dry shirt and fresh Levi's, a maroon sash around her waist adding a note of color. She sat on the edge of the bed and ran a brush through the flame hair, looking delicious doing so.

"You did it, Fargo. I never thought you could. You're a truly remarkable man," Cornelia said as she brushed.

"You wanted me to leave you there. Save yourself, you said," he reminded her with a smile.

She put the brush down. "I'd say it again. It was only right," she said.

"It was selfless of you," he said, and she gave a little shrug and looked away modestly. "But I've a confession to make," he said. "I didn't come get you for the reasons you think." Her brows lifted, and it was his turn for a little shrug, apology in it. "By the way, I took care of the sloops, destroyed all of them. General Beauregard didn't get the message in time. He got there too late to stop me."

"Message? What message?" Cornelia asked.

"Your message," Fargo said.

Cornelia frowned at him. "What are you talking about?"

"It took me a long time to figure it out. In fact, I never really did. I just came onto it," he said.

"You're not making any sense. I don't understand any of this," Cornelia said indignantly.

Fargo's smile was chiding. "Sure you do. The general expected me at the caves. He knew I'd be following tracks. You were the only one who knew I was going back searching in the mountains again. I told you that in the note I left you. Linda didn't know. Joey figured I wasn't even coming back. You were the only one who knew, the only one who could've alerted Beauregard."

Cornelia's face had become a beautiful piece of ice sculpture. "This is preposterous," she hissed.

"It all came together then, all the other things, the big ones and the little ones," Fargo said almost apologetically. "Suddenly, I knew what Kenny Corrigan was really trying to say by the word *double*. He'd found out there was a double agent at work, a very highly placed one. That was you, honey, and you had him hunted down and killed. The other things came to fall into place. Your family was broke, and suddenly you had all the money you needed. The government doesn't pay its agents that much. You were getting paid by both sides, a double agent."

"You're mad," Cornelia flung at him.

"It's true, all of it. You even kept me in bed with you the night the last wagons came through," Fargo said. "And you weren't kidnapped onto the ship. Winslow's man misinterpreted what he saw. The four men with you were protectors, not kidnappers. Things were getting too sticky. Maybe they were afraid you'd be found out, so they called you in before you were uncovered. You agreed it'd be best to seem to be taken away. Aboard the ship you weren't being selfless with me. You were still playing your role. You tried to play the martyr and get rid of me, but it was self-protection, not selflessness."

"Get out. You've gone mad," she screamed.

"Still playing it out, waiting for another chance to disappear," Fargo said, ice coming into his voice. "But it's over. You shouldn't have acted on my note. A professional agent knows there is information you can't act on without revealing yourself. You slipped up on that. But then, you were never a real professional. You were good, and too beautiful for anyone to suspect, but never a real pro."

"Go to hell, Fargo," Cornelia hissed just as the front door opened and John Nicolay strode in, Captain Winslow a pace behind him.

"By God, Cornelia, you're safe," Nicolay said.

"Not exactly," Fargo said, and both men frowned at him.

"Don't listen to him," Cornelia bit out.

Fargo smiled. "Gentlemen, let me introduce you to someone you know but don't know, Cornelia Jeffers, the most beautiful double agent you'll ever find." As Nicolay and Winslow listened, their mouths dropping open, he filled in the picture with the damning details that were beyond denying. Both men stared at Cornelia when he finished, shock in their eyes. "Those twelve agents you said you'd just lost?" Fargo finished. "I'll wager Cornelia can tell you about that."

He turned his eyes on Cornelia and suddenly noticed she had moved just back of Winslow. He started toward her when she pulled the gun out of the maroon sash around her waist and shoved it into the captain's back. A Sharps, four-barreled derringer with rifled barrels, a deadly little weapon at close range. "Outside, walk slowly, Captain," Cornelia said, keeping the derringer into Winslow's back.

"Follow orders, Captain," Fargo said. Cornelia was trapped, and suddenly as desperate as she was beautiful. She wouldn't hesitate to kill. She knew about killing. She arranged, conspired in, and ordered enough killings. Up close would be a new experience for her. But so would a hangman's noose or a firing squad. No, she'd not hesitate for a moment, Fargo knew. He stood quietly by as she disappeared out the door with Winslow. When she was out of sight, he turned to John Nicolay. "There's a back entrance," he said.

"Yes. I'll show you," Nicolay said.

"The stables?"

"Behind the house," the president's secretary said as he ran to the back door with Fargo.

Fargo pulled the door open. "Get back to Mister Lincoln," he said. "I'll come there for you." He slid out the rear door of the town house, but heard hoofbeats galloping away before he reached the stable. He paused, listened, grimaced. Two horses. He'd hoped she'd taken one. Two riders would slow her down. He frowned as he ran around the house to where the Ovaro was tethered outside. With Winslow on his own horse, the derringer wouldn't have the accuracy or firepower she'd need to control him. He reached the Ovaro, still frowning, as Nicolay came out the front door. "Does the captain carry a revolver?" he asked.

"Yes, a Starr, six-shot, double-action Navy revolver," Nicolay said. "He always has it with him."

"Not anymore," Fargo grunted as he swung onto the Ovaro. Cornelia had it now. That's why she'd put Winslow on his own horse. She could easily bring him down with the Starr. Fargo sent the Ovaro a few dozen yards, halted, and leaned over the pinto's neck as he strained his ears. The late night streets of the capital were silent, and he picked up the hoofbeats, then sent the Ovaro into a gallop. Cornelia had made her first mistake. She was staying to the cobbled streets, and that let him pick up the hoofbeats. Fargo found dirt and grass alongside the streets, put the pinto on it, took advantage of a small park, then found another broad and unpaved stretch. Cornelia wasn't very far ahead, the sound of the two horses hard and loud on the stone streets, and he wondered why she was staying on the cobbled streets.

He was coming up close when he ran out of grass and dirt and had to take to the cobblestones. But as he did, he heard the sound of the hoofbeats ahead change character, become duller, not as staccato. He rifled through his mind, and the answer exploded out of stored knowledge. The horses were racing on wood. There were a number of small, wooden bridges across the Potomac, he remembered, and swung the pinto sharply east. The bridge appeared moments later, narrow and low over the water, wood planking with low railings. But the hoofbeats had stopped, and he spurred his horse forward, reached the near end of the bridge, and swung onto the wood planks, then came to an immediate halt.

Cornelia's buckskin and the other horse were standing riderless almost at the other end of the short bridge. Fargo moved the pinto forward slowly, his hand on the butt of the Colt in its holster. The bridge was too narrow for anyone to hide on it, and he steered the Ovaro against the right rail, his eyes searching the edge, peering over it down at the water. He swore softly as he saw nothing, reached the end of the bridge, and swung from the horse. He dropped the Ovaro's reins to the ground and crouched down, peering under the low bridge, his hand on the Colt again. Squinting through the narrow darkness under the bridge, he scanned the water, looking for bobbing heads, wondering if she had gone into the river with the captain. She could also have smashed the heavy Starr on his head and sent him underwater to drown. But that would mean she was through with him as a hostage, and it seemed a little soon for that.

But no bobbing heads surfaced under the bridge. He scanned the heavy stone sides under the wood roadway and swore again as he saw nothing. He was just about to back out of the arched end of the bridge when he spotted a small, flat stone against the wall, river water lapping against it, almost obscuring it. Fargo moved forward again, placed one foot on it, and tested. The stone didn't move, and he brought his other foot onto it. The stones of the bridge curved outward, making him incline his body backward, and he ran both hands across the stones. He stopped suddenly, felt one of the stones move, pressed harder, and the stone turned inward. A larger stone beside it slowly moved and became a narrow entranceway.

Fargo had to squeeze his big frame through the opening, but he managed it and stared at the stone steps that led down to a tunnel. He followed the tunnel, a lantern hanging on the wall lighting the dark passageway. He turned as he heard the stones slide back into place behind him, then continued on through the narrow tunnel. How many spies and secret agents had used this tunnel? he wondered. How many times had Cornelia used it? The tunnel curved slowly, and he smelled the dank dampness of it and strained his ears as well as his eyes. But he heard no voices, no sounds of footsteps, nothing. Suddenly, the wall of stone rose in front him, blocking any exit. He halted and began to slowly run his hands over the stones, pressing each one as he did.

He had reached the center of the wall when he pressed a particularly smooth stone. Instantly, a large stone swung open and a gust of clean air blew into his face. Fargo stepped through the exit and found himself in a thick cluster of dense black willow. He heard the stone close behind him, looked back, and saw the leaves all but hide the stones. He went on, dropped to one knee when he cleared the willows, and spotted the two sets of footprints on soft ground. He rose and followed the prints as they led across a field. He saw scattered houses in the distance, houses that needed paint, had roofs with holes in them, bordered with fences that were broken and leaning. But most had lamps burning inside, people living in them. The footprints continued on, past the houses and across another field, this one dotted with tree clusters.

He saw a house half hidden in a stand of hackberry, a light on in one window, and he dropped to a crouch, then circled to come around at the side of the house. It grew more decrepit as he came closer and moved on silent steps to the window, dropping low to peer inside. He saw Cornelia first, the big Starr in one hand, then found Captain Winslow seated in an armchair in one corner, a trickle of blood running down his temple. Winslow had made a try at escaping and felt the weight of the pistol. But, as often, the scene said more than it appeared to say. It said that Cornelia still wanted a hostage. She could have shot Winslow, but she hadn't.

Fargo gazed over the room—the torn wallpaper, cracked fireplace mantel, a chair with a broken leg. This was no major hideaway house. This was a stopping place for agents on the run, a place to meet and flee, to abandon if necessary. Or, he grimaced, to leave dead bodies behind. But Cornelia had come here, which meant she expected others would stop by. Fargo crept forward to the front of the house. He couldn't wait for that to happen. The odds would be all hers then. But as he moved toward the front door, he halted, dropped to one knee, and cursed as four horsemen came out of the night and reined to a halt in front of the house. Fargo retreated to the window again, saw the men enter, and Cornelia face them. He couldn't hear through the window, but saw Cornelia gesture to the captain. A few minutes more of terse conversation followed, and the four men turned, went to the captain, and pulled him from the chair.

They started for the door with him as Cornelia stayed in the house. One of the men stayed inside with her, Fargo saw, as the others half walked, half dragged Winslow with them. There was no wondering what would happen next. The three men would put an end to the captain, possibly leave him in a field or drop him into one of the small tributaries that branched out from the Potomac. They'd return for Cornelia then. Once again she'd be on her way, but this time she'd be successful. Fargo pulled the Colt from its holster. There was no time left for anything but a fast and furious shoot-out. It was Winslow's only chance to stay alive, and Fargo grunted at the incongruousness.

He rose, stepped to one of the hackberrys, and waited until the men were outside the house. He aimed at one holding onto the captain, fired, and the man flew backward as if he'd been kicked by an invisible mule. The others spun, drew their weapons, and Fargo saw Winslow throw himself to the ground. The Colt barked again, twice, and both men staggered, legs turning into rubber, their shots going harmlessly into the air. Both fell at once, hit into each other as they did, and lay still, legs entangled on the ground. The door of the house flew open, and the fourth man ran out, gun in hand, staring at the three forms on the ground as he halted, the open doorway at his back.

"Don't move, or you're next," Fargo said. "Drop the gun."

The man pulled his eyes from the three figures so still on the ground and let his gun fall. "Don't shoot," he said.

"That's smart," Fargo said. "You'll live, and even duck a firing squad if you tell us everything you know."

"Anything," the man said. "I'm no damn hero." Fargo saw Winslow getting to his feet as he started toward the man in the doorway.

"Good," Fargo grunted when a shot exploded. The man's eyes grew wide as his body shook, and he staggered forward, pain, shock, betrayal, and realization all passing through his bulging eyes. A bubble of blood came to his mouth as he fell forward, hitting the ground facedown, and Fargo saw the gaping stain of red in the middle of his back. He also heard a rear door slam, and he cursed as he ran around the house, pushed through trees, and slowed as he saw the thick foliage and high brush behind the house. "It's no use, Cornelia," he shouted. "Give up. It's over." A shot answered him that grazed his ear, and he dropped low, flattening himself as another shot just missed him.

He peered at the high brush and searched for movement, but she was still as a church mouse. He started to push to his knees, then dove forward as a shot grazed his shoulder. She had passed desperation. She had crossed into another dimension made of contradictions and emotions escalating out of control—anger, remorse, ambition, and fear—a kind of madness that grew of itself and consumed reason. The big, exciting game without convictions or principles, the head-spinning power of outwitting everyone, had turned sour. The glorious beauty that was such an asset, such a tool and so wonderful to use, had more and more served death and the grasping concerns of others. An inner corrosion had overtaken Cornelia, excess leading to excess until there was no stopping, until there was only the self. There is a reason for convictions, principles, loyalties, Cornelia was proving. Without them there is no need for caring, for believing in anything or anyone. Without them there is nothingness.

And now she was beyond reason, beyond remorse. Now she was like a crazed beast, caring only about survival, willing to stop at nothing for that. He swore at the climate that had brought this into being. There wasn't even a war, yet its shadows were already turning and twisting the minds of men and women. Cornelia didn't reflect what had been, he feared, but what was to come. He started to slide along the ground, and another shot came. But he caught the movement in the high brush this time. He counted her fourth shot, brought the Colt up, and fired where the brush had moved. He heard her snort of anger, and two more shots hit only inches from him.

"That's the sixth shot," he called out and started to push to his feet. "Come out. It's over, dammit."

A quick fusillade of bullets cut through the air, all of them wide of their mark as he dived to the ground, rolled, and came up against a tree. *Damn*, he swore.

He'd forgotten about the derringer. But he pushed to his feet again and hoped he hadn't forgotten about anything else. "It's really over now," he called. He saw the high brush move, and she stepped out, holding the big Starr in one hand, the derringer in the other. She glared at him for a moment, then turned and began to run, faster than he'd expected she could. "Stop," he called, and started after her, wondering if he had counted correctly. She spun suddenly and raised both guns. He skidded to a halt and flung himself sideways. He heard the shot ring out as he hit the ground, then turned to see Cornelia standing still, a red stain spreading across her white shirt, instantly covering all of her chest.

She looked at him as she slowly sank to the ground, both guns falling from her fingers. Fargo turned and saw the captain behind him, the gun in his hand. "Took it from one of her friends," Winslow said. Fargo holstered the Colt and stepped to where Cornelia lay, the agate green eyes lifeless yet somehow still magnetic. The red stain matched her hair, he found himself thinking, then heard Winslow come up beside him.

"I figured to bring her in alive," Fargo said.

"To a firing squad or a hangman's rope? Would that be any better?" Winslow asked. Fargo said nothing. He had no answer for the question. He bent down and looked at the Starr and the derringer. They were both empty.

"I think that's what she felt," he said, turned, and slowly walked away.

16

Winslow caught up to him, and they walked together, neither man saying anything. When they reached the bridge over the Potomac, Fargo gathered in the Ovaro, and Winslow rode with him back to the house in the capital as the new day came. John Nicolay hurried down to see them, and Fargo let the captain tell him what had happened, then took over to fill him in on the tunnel and the house.

"I'll have our people see to both places. We'll close down the tunnel and burn down the house," Nicolay said. He paused and looked uncomfortably at Fargo. "There's still that attempt on President Lincoln's life. We haven't been able to find out a thing—who, where, when. But as I told you, we've lost twelve of our top agents."

"You want me to have a crack at it?" Fargo said.

"I'd feel a lot better if you did," Nicolay said.

"A trailsman needs something to trail—tracks, prints, signs, something, if only a region, but someplace to start. You've nothing, no clues, no leads, only rumors," Fargo said.

"You're right," John Nicolay said unhappily. "I just need to do something, to try to avoid an attempt on the president's life. Helplessness is a terrible feeling. Somebody has to know something."

"Yes, those who are going to do it," Winslow said.

"You're saying we can't stop them," Nicolay said. Winslow nodded gravely. "We can only hope they'll fail."

Fargo frowned into space as the two men talked, his thoughts racing. "I'll wager somebody knew, somebody who no doubt communicated with them, somebody who had a thumb on everything that went on."

"Cornelia," Nicolay breathed, and Fargo nodded.

"She's not able to help us, so there's nobody," the captain said.

"Help can come in funny ways," Fargo said. "I need a few hours shut-eye. Then have four of your men meet me at the Jeffers town house."

"You can rest in one of the guest rooms upstairs," Nicolay said. "And I'll have the men ready when you wake."

Fargo shrugged acceptance, happy not to have to look for a place to bed down. He was shown to an opulent guest room with presidential seals on the sheets and slept quickly, glad to close out the night. When he woke and went downstairs, he found breakfast waiting for him and four young soldiers. He ate hungrily, then took the mug of coffee with him as he went to Cornelia's town house. He made a place for himself in the study, settled in behind a big desk, and faced the four soldiers. "I want you to search this house from top to bottom and bring me every piece of paper, notebook, diary, envelope, and parchment you can find. Anything that has writing on it—words, numbers, short, long, clear, unclear. I want you to pay special attention to anything in the bedrooms, studies, desks, drawers, bathrooms. Go through the laundry, too. Is that clear?"

"Yes, sir," one of the soldier said, and led the others up the stairs. "We'll start at the top, sir," he called back.

"Start wherever you want. I'll do this room," Fargo said, and began pulling out desk drawers. He found a lot of notes, accounts, ledgers, diarylike pads, went through each page of each item carefully. The soldiers brought him plenty, yet not as much as he'd expected there might be. It was night when he'd gone through every single scrap of paper, studied each of them, and rejected every single one as having no importance for him. When he finished, he had a small, single sheet of paper on the desk in front of him, its words written in ink.

He dismissed the soldiers, put the slip of paper in his pocket, and went to the official presidential residence, where John Nicolay greeted him with a bourbon. Nicolay frowned at the slip of paper when Fargo showed it to him. "Why in God's name do you attach any importance to this?" the president's secretary asked.

"It was found in her bedroom, under a drawer full of scarves and kerchiefs, not a place you'd keep an address," Fargo said. "It's the only thing in the house, the only piece of paper in the house that has no connection with anything else. Most every other address, name, note, reference can be connected, explained, or related to something—friends, guests, merchants, other correspondence. The name and address on this piece of paper do not show up anywhere else, not on any other list, note, or reference. I'm going to find out why."

"There's more than one way to read a trail, isn't there," John Nicolay murmured. "You want anyone with you?"

"No. I'm going alone," Fargo said.

Nicolay glanced at the slip of paper again. "This address isn't that far away. It's in the Culpeper area," he said.

"I know. That's another thing that bothers me about it. Every other social address she had is for people close by here in Washington or people real far away. This address is just far enough to be out of range and close enough to get here quickly," Fargo said.

"Good luck," Nicolay said.

Fargo left with a warm handshake, climbed onto the Ovaro, and rode from the capital, heading southwest. He rode across rolling hills, napped for a few hours when the moon was high, and rode again before the dawn. The noon sun had gone its way when he reached the Culpeper area, and he halted, then took the slip of paper from his pocket.

"Mary Sanders, #3 Kingdom Road, Culpeper

Ridge," he read aloud, pushed the slip back into his pocket, and stopped at a peanut farmer for directions.

"Yep, I know the place. Go east up this road," the farmer said. "But go easy. Folks up there don't like strangers."

"All the folks up there?" Fargo queried.

"No, just the ones on Kingdom Road," the man said, and Fargo rode on with an appreciative nod. He found Culpeper Ridge, which turned out to be a wide stretch of land, far too wide to deserve the term *ridge*. Strong growths of box elder covered the land, and as the day began to turn to dusk, Fargo moved slowly along Kingdom Road. When dark had descended, he moved more quickly, then slowed again as he heard voices and smelled freshly brewed coffee. Dismounting, he took the big Henry and went on foot, saw lights twinkle ahead, and the voices grew stronger as did the smell of the coffee. A house came into sight, bulky with a steep roof. A lamp hung from the open front door and lighted the wooden 3 nailed above the door.

Fargo crept closer and saw two big dead-axle drays with extra heavy brakes alongside the house, four men with rifles alongside the wagons, some sipping coffee from metal cups. Fargo peered at the wagons again. Both were loaded with casks. He studied the casks for another long moment. Beer casks, he saw, a furrow creasing his brow. Why were four armed guards with two big wagons of beer barrels? And what were they doing up in this isolated, forsaken place? He circled, came up along the rear of the house, crept to the partly open window at the side, and peered in. Three men were crouched around a low table, their backs to the window, where a large kerosene lamp burned. It illuminated a large, crudely drawn map hung on the wall. A building became recognizable, and below it the heavy letters printed: No. 14, INDEPENDENCE AVENUE. Beside the building, one on each side, were the two wagons loaded with the beer barrels.

Fargo frowned at the picture, and he lowered himself so he could hear the men at the table. "I'll not wait any longer. This was planned for months, every part of it planned carefully. The great Mister Lincoln will be addressing a gathering inside number fourteen. We'll have the wagons outside. When he comes out, we'll give him a welcome he's never had and never will have again," the man said. "But we can't wait any longer. They haven't got word to us, so we'll have to go on our own." One of the men raised his voice and called. A lanky figure came into the room, a boy not much more than twenty-five. "Rawley, you have your orders," the man at the table said without really turning around. "You and your brother start for Washington a little before dawn. That'll get you there with the wagons before the address is over and the president leaves the building. Soon as you see him come from the building, leap from your wagons and run."

Fargo stared at the beer barrels again. An attempt on the president's life made with beer barrels? It didn't make any sense. But it was clearly a plot against the president, one Cornelia had known about, the address of the plotters in her house, hidden under the kerchiefs in her bedroom dresser. His thoughts were interrupted as the three men rose, their backs still to him, and strode to the door. "We'll leave now, Rawley," one of the men said. "See you both tomorrow." Fargo stayed flattened beneath the window as the three men left, their backs still to him. They climbed into a buggy with a rumble seat and drove away.

Fargo moved from the window and saw the young man they'd called Rawley go to a boy who could've been his twin, and both talked in quiet, tight voices. Finally, Rawley left his brother and wandered closer, sitting down against a thick tree trunk. Fargo felt his uneasiness stirring into a turmoil. Something was going to happen that didn't seem to make any sense, and the answers were under his nose. He'd find out, he told himself, and laid the rifle on the ground and took out the Colt. Silently, he crept up behind the young man, pressing the barrel of the Colt against his forehead while he wrapped one arm around his neck.

"Shhhhh," Fargo whispered. "Noise makes this gun go off. Just come with me." Moving backward, his arm tight around the youth's neck, he dragged Rawley into the thick of the trees. Taking his arm away, he moved the Colt and let Rawley stare at it as the gun pointed at his face. "That's your brother you were talking to, right?" Fargo asked, and the boy nodded. "I'll blow his head off in a split second unless you tell me what I want to know," Fargo said, his voice low, calm, almost matter-of-fact. Rawley stared at him with a panic in his eyes. But Fargo saw he harnessed the panic and had enough presence to mount a reply.

"What're you gonna do after I tell you? Shoot him anyway?"

"No. I don't play that way," Fargo said. "What's going on here, and what's your part in it?"

"Roscoe and me, they hired us. That's all we have to do with it. We don't want anything more with it. We just need the money," Rawley said.

Fargo nodded. The answer was one he had concluded for himself. "Now what's the rest? Why are you driving two wagons full of beer cases to where the president's going to come out of a meeting? Why all the way from Culpeper when he could get beer right in Washington? Now that doesn't seem to make any sense, does it, Rawley?"

"No, mister, it doesn't." Rawley swallowed.

Fargo's eyes hardened on the youth. "What's in those beer casks, Rawley?" he asked.

"Gunpowder," Rawley said very softly.

Fargo's eyes stayed on the youth as did the Colt, as he let the enormity of the single word sweep through him. *Gunpowder*. Gunpowder disguised as beer casks, enough to blow up everyone anywhere near the building, outside and inside. But of course the plotters were interested in killing only one person. Everyone else would be sacrificed for their objective. Fargo felt almost sick at the staggering knowledge that it had been carefully plotted to succeed with absolute certainty. It hadn't been conceived in haste, planned casually. It had taken months to come up with the right date, the right moment, to gather all the beer casks and fill them with gunpowder.

The plotters were no wild-eyed, bourbon-driven hotheads. They were zealots, twisted perhaps, but nonetheless zealots. Their goals wouldn't be turned aside, not by one failure, not by more than one. But he'd start with one failure, Fargo told himself. He'd push them back, make them start over again for another time that might never come. He turned off his thoughts, Rawley watching him apprehensively. "I've some more questions, but they'll wait till later," Fargo said to the youth. "Call your brother over here. Don't try anything stupid. Just call him over."

"Yes, sir." Rawley nodded and raised his voice, calling out to Roscoe. "That's right, over here," Rawley reiterated. Fargo watched Roscoe approach and peer into the trees, frowning. "In here, dammit," Rawley said, and Roscoe pushed his way into the trees, stopping in his tracks as he saw the rifle pointed at him. "The man says he means us no harm. We'd best take his word for it," Rawley told his brother.

"Listen to Rawley," Fargo said. "Lie down, both of you, cover your ears." Both brothers obeyed, and Fargo stepped back. "What about the four guards by the wagons? They just hired hands, too?" Fargo asked.

"They're kinfolk," Rawley said.

"Of the men who just left?" Fargo asked, and both youths nodded. "Too bad," Fargo muttered, then flattened himself on the ground behind Rawley and

Roscoe, raised the rifle, and sighted through the dense foliage. He knew he'd only need one shot in one wagon, but he fired off two, just to be safe, dropped the rifle at his side, and put his head down.

The earth shook, the trees quivering, and the night sky became red and yellow and orange. The wagons and the beer casks vanished into the night. Fargo glimpsed two sailing skyward still intact. The house disappeared, a mass of flying lumber that sailed in all directions. When the tremendous explosion died away, the gray-white smoke rose and swirled upward, partly caught in a wind of its own making. Fargo rose onto one knee, the rifle in hand, and peered from the trees. Small, isolated fires gave enough light to show that there was a shallow crater where the house had been. Fargo saw a wagon wheel embedded in the trunk of a big box elder. Slowly, he pushed to his feet as the trees still shimmered and rustled. He watched Rawley and Roscoe get up, their faces pale and filled with fear.

"I want names, and I'll let you boys go home in one piece. Who were the men that left?" he queried.

"Lewis Powell. He sometimes calls himself Payne," Rawley said. "David Herold and George Atzerodt, a Dutchman."

"Is there anybody else?" Fargo pressed.

"Yes, he came and they all looked up to him. But he never told me his name, never used it except when he was alone with the others," Rawley said.

"What'd he look like? Describe him," Fargo said.

"Average height, on the thin side, mustache."

"Nothing else?"

"He's a good talker, big voice, walks back and forth when he talks, waves his arms like an actor on a stage," Rawley said.

"You never heard anyone call him by name?" Fargo asked.

"David Herold called him John, once."

"What about the house? How'd they get that? Fargo questioned.

"A woman friend of theirs rented it for them to use," Rawley said. "She goes under the name Mary Sanders, sometimes Mary Brown, but those aren't her real name."

"How do you know?"

"Saw her sign the rental papers for the house. Her name's Mary Surratt. She also runs a boardinghouse they use. I don't know where," Rawley said.

Fargo holstered the Colt. "You've earned your skins," he said. "Be more careful who you work for next time."

Both youths nodded and hurried away, not looking back. Fargo returned to the Ovaro and rode back to Washington, not hurrying. It was midmorning when he faced John Nicolay and found Abraham Lincoln there. Both men listened to everything he told them, their faces both relieved and depressed. "It'll take them a good spell to concoct another plot," he said. "But they're out there. They'll keep trying, I'm afraid. They're mad zealots, especially the one called John. Maybe you can get a lead on him from the description I gave you."

Abraham Lincoln gave one of his rare smiles. "That description could fit most of the flowery congressmen in Washington," he said. "They all wave their arms and pace back and forth."

"We'll look for the ones whose names you gave us. But if they're in secessionist states, it'll be hard to get at them," John Nicolay said.

The tall figure stepped forward and extended his hand to Fargo. "You've done everything we wanted of you and so much more. If the Union is preserved, you'll have played a real part in it, Fargo."

"And if it isn't?" Fargo asked.

"Then all you've done will not have been enough, just as all I've done will have failed. You could say we'll have failed together," Lincoln said.

"It's better to fail with some people than win with others," Fargo said. The tall, gaunt figure was still standing in the center of the room as he left, somehow looking both strong and vulnerable.

17

The hollow was filled with crates and boxes, tools and bags, figures hurrying back and forth carrying more things as a squad from the Sixth Regiment unloaded the wagons unable to come in any closer. Fargo found Joey beside him, clinging to his hand, while Zeke Cole and Zed Crabble looked on, the others watching and helping with a combination of joy and surprise. "You came back," Joey said. "I wondered if you would, if you could."

"Keeping your promise, too, mister. We put real store in keeping promises here in the Shenandoah," Zeke Cole said.

"You did your part," Fargo said, and went with Joey as she pulled him aside. "Can you stay?" she asked eagerly. "For the night?" He smiled. Her smoldering sensuality hadn't diminished any.

"Sorry," he said. "Got some other stops to make on my way west." He searched her face and saw that nothing had changed in the unvarnished openness of her, either. "You take care of yourself," he said, finding words suddenly difficult to choose.

Her little smile held an edge of sly wisdom. "If things turn out the way I want, I'll have something to hold," she said.

"And if they don't?"

"I'll have something to remember. Either way I win," she said. He turned, and she walked from the hollow with him, then stopped as he pulled himself onto the Ovaro. She kissed him, lips soft and throbbing, pulled away, and ran, disappearing into the hollow. Her mountain world, their mountain world, he mused as he rode. He once thought it a backwater of the world outside, a place turned in on itself with nothing to offer. He wasn't sure any longer. Maybe there was a wisdom in simplicity that other world had lost.

He turned the pinto south, stayed in the long, thickly covered spine of the Appalachians, and some four mornings later he made his way into the Cumberland, up into the high land, finally to halt where a wide stretch of clay pots bordered the sturdy cabin. Linda came out as he dismounted, a soft yellow shirt echoing the dark blond, short hair. "Didn't expect me, did you?" He smiled.

"I wondered plenty," she said.

"That's being honest." He laughed and went into the cabin with her, taking in the way her small rear moved and the sharp upturn of her breasts, and he remembered all the contradictory excitement of her. She brought out a bottle of bourbon, and two glasses and set them down.

"You going to make me wait more? I figure I've waited enough," she said, poured the bourbon, and gave him a glass.

"You have," he said, sat back, and began by telling her what Kenny had meant by his last word, *double*. The rest followed of itself, and he recounted everything about Cornelia, down to the very last of it. Linda sat quietly when he finished, staring into space for a long time.

"Knowing helps," she said finally. "Feeling empty is better than feeling angry." She fell silent for another moment. "Is there going to be a war?" she asked.

He shrugged. "Can't say. It's awfully close. What'll you do if it happens? Stay here with your plants?"

"You mean hide?" She smiled. "I don't know that I could do that, being a Virginia girl born and bred. But I won't help them with their war, not after they killed Kenny. I'll work in a hospital, something like that. I'm sure they'll be needing plenty of help."

"You can count on that," he agreed.

"Where will you be, Fargo, back in your mountains and prairies?" she asked.

"Yes, trying to open new lands while the old ones are tearing themselves apart. Sounds pretty ridiculous, doesn't it?" he reflected.

"I know something that's more ridiculous," she said, and he waited. "Your going away without another night together, maybe more than one."

"That'd be plain stupid, wouldn't it?" he agreed.

Linda began to unbutton her shirt, flicked open the last button, and the saucy, upturned little breasts pushed forward at once. He gathered them into his arms. His mountain and prairies could wait. Loving was where you found it. Pleasure had no borders.